Fear My Gangsta

Tranay Adams

**Lock Down Publications and Ca$h
Presents**
Fear My Gangsta
A Novel by *Tranay Adams*

Lock Down Publications
P.O. Box 870494
Mesquite, Tx 75187

Visit our website @
www.lockdownpublications.com

Copyright Fear My Gangsta

First Edition 2015
Printed in the United States of America

This is a work of fiction. Names, characters, places, and incidents either are products of the author's imagination or are used fictitiously. Any similarity to actual events or locales or persons, living or dead, is entirely coincidental.

Lock Down Publications
Like our page on Facebook: Lock Down Publications @
www.facebook.com/lockdownpublications.ldp
Cover design and layout by: **Dynasty Cover Me**
Book interior design by: **Shawn Walker**
Edited by: **Jasmine Devonish**

Stay Connected with Us!

Text **LOCKDOWN** to 22828 to stay up-to-date with new releases,
sneak peaks, contests and more…
Or **CLICK HERE** to sign up.
Thank you.

Like our page on Facebook:

Lock Down Publications: Facebook

Join Lock Down Publications/The New Era Reading Group

Visit our website @
www.lockdownpublications.com

Follow us on Instagram:

Lock Down Publications: Instagram

Email Us: We want to hear from you!

I done walked in a killa shoes, a drug dealer shoes...

B.G-*Made Man*

CHAPTER ONE
2003

They call me the Don Dada, pop a collar/ Drop a dollar if you hear me, you can holla/ Even Rottweilers, follow, the Impala/ Wanna talk about this concrete? Nigga, I'm a scholar/ The incredible, hetero sexual, credible/ Beg a hoe, let it go, dick ain't edible/ Nigga ain't federal, I plan shit/ While you handpicked motherfuckers givin' up transcripts...

A cherry red Jeep Cherokee sitting on gold Dayton's bumping NWA's Hello pulled up in front of a white two story house with a rich green manicured lawn. The front passenger door was thrown open. A short nigga rocking a red hoodie and matching sweatpants hopped out. He slammed the door shut and slapped hands with the driver before jogging towards the house. The truck drove off taking the sound of the music along with it. Reaching the porch of his house, the little nigga pulled a bottle of Visine from out of his pocket and dropped a couple of drips into his hooded, red webbed eyes. He blinked his eyes and capped the tiny plastic bottle, slipping it back into his pocket. He then whipped out a personal size bottle of Polo cologne and sprayed himself. Tucking the cologne into his pocket, he pulled out his keys and opened the door. He closed the door shut behind him as he entered the house, pulling the hood from his 360 waves. He locked the door and when he turned around, the living room light came on. His mother and father were sitting at the kitchen table. Lying upon it was a Glock .9mm, a couple of Ziplocs of weed, three bankrolls of money secured by rubber-bands and an ounce of crack. When Fear saw this, he looked away cursing under his breath, fuck. He didn't know what kind of bullshit that he was going to try to feed his parents. Big Al and Verna Simpson were far from dumb.

Al Sr. snatched up the freezer bag of crack and held it up, face balled up in a frown. "What is this?"

"Come on now, pop, you know what it is." Fear blew hard and rolled his eyes, not in the mood for his one of his father's lectures.

"I know what it is, boy. I asked you," Big Al asked angrily, temples pulsating. "Now what is it?"

"Pop."

"Junior, if you force me to get up outta this chair, so help me I'll…," he closed his eyes and massaged the bridge of his nose, trying to keep himself from blowing his top. "Father, give me the strength to get through to this knuckleheaded son of mine, please." He looked up at the ceiling then looked back down at his offspring. "I'ma try this again since I'm starting to lose my temper." He took a couple deep breaths and continued, "What. Is. This?" he shook the freezer bag in his face, startling the pretty green buds with the purple crystals sprinkled upon them.

Fear looked away and licked his lips. Looking defeated, he turned back around and said, "Weed."

"Right. Now tell me what it's doing in my house."

Fear shrugged and said, "I don't know."

"You don't know?" He looked at him as if he was losing his mind. "Boy, are you trying to insult my intelligence? We found all of this stuff in your closet." He jabbed a plump finger at him.

"Right. So why were y'all going through my stuff?" he said a little too sharply for his father's taste.

The old man rose to his feet, pulled off his glasses and tucked them into his breast pocket.

"You betta watch your tone and delivery in here, son. 'Cause I'ma 'bout a minute past being on you like stink on shit!" he grumbled heatedly with glassy eyes. He was about to start in his direction until his wife stepped in his path, taking hold of both of his arms trying to calm him down.

"Alvin, calm down," she pleaded, fearing things taking a turn for the worse between the two most important men in her life.

"I didn't mean no disrespect, pop, but y'all treat me like a kid and I'm eighteen now," he pled his case, telling them just how he felt. "I don't have any privacy here. Sometimes I feel like I can't breathe, it's like you and ma are suffocating me."

"Suffocating you?" Al angled his head as lines formed across his forehead. It was like he couldn't believe what he'd just heard. "Son, do you know how good that chu got it? Brand new Benz in the driveway, a wardrobe of clothes, sneakers, big screen TV…this enormous house." His eyes and his massive arms swept around the room briefly. He looked back to his son and said, "You're living like a king, junior, a mothafucking king. Your mother and I saw to it that you had a better life than we've ever had. And you think we're suffocating you? There are kids out there in those streets…" He pointed at the door. "That would die to be in your shoes."

"I hear what chu saying, and I appreciate all that you and ma have provided for me, but I don't quite see the vision y'all have for me."

Al and Verna exchanged glances and then they looked back to their son.

"AJ, what do you mean?" Verna's brows furrowed, wondering what her son was getting at.

"I'm not going to college."

"The hell you aren't," Al grumbled, scowling and nostrils flaring. "You're riding with a full scholarship and your ass is going. That's for goddamn sure!"

"Alvin, don't use the Lord's name in vain."

"I'm sorry baby, but the Lord knows my heart," a hostile Al claimed, "He sees I'm tryna get through to my son."

"I'm sorry, pop, but I'm not going." Fear stood his ground. With that said, Al stalked towards his baby boy and towered over him, threateningly. He looked down upon him with anger glinting in his eyes and his jaws pulsating. His thick hands were balled into fists; he clenched and unclenched them. Fear matched his father's glare as his hot breath ruffling his eyebrows. His pop was the only man in the world he was afraid of but he wouldn't let it show. His old man had always taught him to look a man in the eyes and to never under any circumstances show fear.

"What did you say?" his nostrils flared and his breaths were husky.

"I said I'm not going, pop," he spoke back defiantly, prepared for what would happen next.

Verna oozed between the two men and pushed her husband back. She wasn't nearly strong enough to move him, but he willingly allowed her to move him for fear of what he may do to his only son. His eyes were still locked in a gaze with his boy and his nostrils were still flaring like he was dying to get a shot at his ass.

"Alvin, please, let me talk to him," Verna told her husband. Seeing that he wasn't resisting, she turned to their son. "Baby, why don't chu wanna go to school? I thought we'd all agreed that..."

"No, ma," Fear shook his head. "We didn't agree that I was going to school. You and pop made that decision without my input. I didn't get a say in the matter. In fact, I never get a say in anything. I'm like a puppet...moving every which way that y'all want me to go." He danced around like a limp puppet on strings.

"Why is it that you haven't said anything?" his mother's brows wrinkled.

"How can I? You and pop never let me get a word in edge wise," Fear told her. "Y'all had y'all hearts dead set on UCLA and I didn't have the nerve to tell you that I wasn't going."

Verna thought on it for a time before looking back up at her son. "Alright, AJ, if you don't wanna go to UCLA, then what other school do you wanna go to?"

"Ma, I don't wanna go to school...period."

"What?!" Al snapped, looking at his offspring as if he was a wart growing on his dick.

"School isn't for me...I've got something else in mind." He folded his arms across his chest.

"Oh yeah, Mr. Know It All? Like what?"

Fear looked away and shrugged. Turning back around he said, "I'm sick of school. I was thinking I'd take a couple years off to see exactly what it is that I wanna do."

"Like what? Running around on the East Side with your fool ass cousins, Wameek and Malik, playing gangsta?" Al fumed, his chest expanding and deflating as he breathed heavily.

"Oh, I ain't playing no mo', pop, I got my officials." He licked his thumb and dragged it down the side of his right eye, smearing the skin blending makeup. He revealed a red teardrop tattoo. This meant that he'd murdered someone.

"Noooo," Verna hollered out like Fear had been shot dead in front of her. Mortified, she cupped her hands over her mouth and began to weep, body shuddering hard. Tears accumulated in her eyes and blurred her vision before escaping down her cheeks.

"Junior, Junior, Junior," Al shook his head shamefully, massaging the bridge of his nose. "What have you done? What. Have. You. Done?"

"This is me, pop, this is who I am," Fear stated proudly.

"You've marked yourself for life, boy; you can't wash your hands of the act that you've committed." Al ushered his wife over to the couch. He then took a glass down from the cupboard and filled it with faucet water. He passed it to her and she took a drink.

"I thought your Lord was a merciful one?"

His father shot him a look that he read as You better watch it now, boy!

Fear smirked and turned around to his mother, frowning having seen the sorrowful look on her face. "You alright, ma?" He sat down beside her, taking her hand into his own. He was genuinely concerned about the welfare of the woman that had carried him inside of her belly for nine months.

She passed her husband the glass and turned to her son, caressing the side of his face. She looked into his eyes as tears danced in her own. "Momma's fine, baby, we're gonna pray to the Lord tonight and ask him for your forgiveness, okay?"

Fear nodded. He wasn't too big on God but right then he was willing to go along with anything to pacify his mother.

Hearing something heavy hit the floor drew his and his mother's attention. They saw his father with two duffle bags lying at his feet. He had a very stern yet serious face.

"I want you take your things and leave my home right this minute."

Fear's face balled up hearing his father say that. It had taken him off guard. He'd expected to be punished in some way, but never did he think his old man would go so far as to throw him out on his ass.

He rose to his feet looking pitiful. "Pop, I…"

"Go." He pointed at the door.

"Ma…" Fear turned to his mother and she looked away, grimacing as tears stream down her face. "Alright." He nodded, a ball of hurt had manifested in his chest but he kept a straight face. Although he'd become glassy eyed and wanted to unleash his tears, he wouldn't allow it to fall. He couldn't let his old man know that he'd gotten to him. "If y'all want me to go, then I'll go." He kissed his mother on the cheek and picked up his duffle bags. He lumbered toward the door, slowly stepping as if his ankles were shackled to something that was holding him back.

Verna jumped to her feet and ran over to her husband. "Al, don't give up on our boy, don't let him go. It's a jungle out there in those streets. If he gets hurt or killed I'll just die…I just know I will. Please." She hugged him and laid her face against his torso sobbing. He looked from his grieving wife and his son as he headed for the door, caressing her back lovingly. His lips parted to say something but a thought held him back, he shook his head no.

"I'm sorry baby, but if Junior can't abide by my rules than he can't live under my roof." He stood his ground. Even though he didn't want his baby boy to go either, he felt like it was for the best and that he was teaching him a lesson. He figured that he'd be back in due time once he saw how hard it was out there, but little did he know that his offspring could adapt to any circumstances and environments. He was smart, cunning, clever and witty, so he'd be okay. Not only that he had to survive to show his old man that he could do without him and his money.

The last thing the Simpsons saw of their son was his back when he left out of the door. With a heavy head and an aching heart, he left the house determined to show them that he could manage on his own.

Tranay Adams

CHAPTER TWO
2003

Fear walked down the sidewalk toting his duffle bag and scrolling through recent calls on his cell phone. Once he found the number that he was looking for, he tapped it and the device instantly dialed it up. He placed the cellular to his ear and listened to the line ring until someone answered.

"Yo' I need you to scoop me up Talia," he spoke into the device.

"Something wrong?" She could hear the pain in his voice.

"Nah, pop kicked a nigga outta the house."

"Why? What happened?"

He took a deep breath and gave her the rundown. While he was talking, she was getting dressed to come and get him.

"Fuck you goin'?" A deep ass voice from the other side of the phone said.

"Damn, nigga, you all up in mine, gon' get chu some," Italia spoke like a hood rat, sounding disgruntled.

"Who you talkin' to?" Homeboy got belligerent.

"You nigga!" She spat back with the fury of an AK-47.

Fear grinned, imagining her moving her head like chicken heads in the hood do. For as bourgeois as she was, she could go from classy to ratchet real quick. Most thought that Italia was born and raised in Calabasas, but really she was straight out of Compton. The truth was she was all about her grips. She fucked with ballers and get money niggaz and that was it. Little momma didn't have any holler for dudes that weren't holding. Niggaz had to pay if they wanted to play. And pay they did because she was just that fine. Italia used her earnings to live the lavish life. At nineteen, she had her own Malibu beach house, a fly ass 7 series Beemer and a Kawasaki Ninja motorcycle. The fine mothafucka stayed in the latest fashion. Her neck and wrists stayed draped in diamonds and gold. I Ain't saying she a gold digger but she ain't messing with no broke niggaz.

"Bitch, I'll raise up off this bed and beat cho mothafuckin' ass!"

"Hold on, bae," Italia told Fear and he heard her set the cordless telephone down. There was rummaging through and then a Click! Clack!

"Hold up, baby!" homeboy cowered.

Hearing old boy bitch up caused a smile to form across Fear's face. No matter how uppity his homegirl seemed she was still as hood as mini motorbikes and sneakers hanging from a power line.

"Oh, now I'm baby? Nigga, get cho shit and raise up outta mine 'fore I baptize you."

"Alright, damn." A moment later he heard a door slam shut.

Italia cleared her throat and cooed into the receiver sweetly. "Hello?"

"You straight over there, ma?" he cracked a grin. He wasn't the least bit worried about her wellbeing. She was a straight up G and could handle hers.

"Yeah, I'm good. So what happened?" she asked concerned.

"I'll explain everything once you get here."

"Okay, gimmie about…" she paused and he assumed she glanced at the clock. "Thirty minutes, okay?"

"Alright. I'll see you then." He disconnected the call and slid the cell into his pocket.

Thirty Minutes later

Italia pulled up in a navy blue BMW 760 in thirty minutes just like she said she would. Fear hopped into the front passenger seat and slammed the door shut.

"'Sup, handsome?" She smiled and dimples indented her cheeks.

"'Sup?" He leaned forward and kissed her cheek.

She drove off with Usher's Bad Girl playing softly from her speakers.

Italia was a mahogany complexion beauty with soft brown eyes and wavy shoulder length hair. She was what you would call a skinny thick chick. Her curves began at her thighs. She had two palms full of breasts and an ass like an Atlanta stripper.

"You okay, baby?" Italia glanced over at him, seeing the bewildered look on his face. She took her French tipped fingers and slid them down and around his face. Her delicate touch seemed to calm the beast inside of him. When he closed his eyes he could feel it in him growling like a tiger having its stomach massaged. Purrrrr! He leaned his head to the side, rubbing his cheek up against her palm.

"I'll be fine, especially if I get my medicine." He peeled his eyelids open and looked up at her with a knowing grin. He was talking about getting some pussy from her that night. He felt bad about what had went down between him and his parents, but he knew that once he slid up in something warm, wet and tight all of his worries would be zapped right out of him.

"Well," she began grinning and taking his hand, sliding it up her thigh. The further his palm traveled the more intense the warmth became until he was right by her hot, moist pussy. "If you play your cards right, then you may get lucky."

"Mmmm." He shut his eyes and rubbed her V through her damp panties. The temperature that it exhausted felt like that of a sauna. He licked his lips imagining what it would be like to be inside of her again, feeling the soft interior of her sex hugging his dick like a pair of hands. "Aww, damn." Although Italia and Fear wasn't officially together, they fucked around like they were. Truthfully, he was the only nigga that she played close that she wasn't making kick her down. She fucked with him heavy though. The only thing that stopped them from placing labels on one another was that they were focused on running their bands up and felt like a relationship would just complicate things. Other than that, they were good with one another. When they were together nothing or no one else existed or mattered outside of their union. That's just the way that they liked it.

Fear peeled his eyelids back open and said, "Pull over."

She smiled excitedly showcasing her pearly whites. "Where?"

"Anywhere," he slid his hand inside of his sweats and molested his hardness. Her eyes darted to his lap and she bit down on her inner jaw, anticipating feeling all of that meat spearing her center.

"Alright, I got chu faded, boo." She slipped her gentle hand inside of his sweats and groped his grown man, causing him to throw his head back and squirm in his seat. Her delicate touch made his shit expand slightly in girth and width. Italia looked from her conquest's pleasured face as she was glancing to the windshield. She spotted the perfect spot for them to duck off and get their freak on. A few houses down there was a house with a For Rent sign on its front lawn which meant no one would be there. She was going to drive up into the driveway and into the backyard so that they could get busy.

"Sssssss, oh, shit." Fear pressed one hand up against the ceiling while his other gripped the door handle. His ass rose from the seat feeling her hand massage his dick, sliding the skin of it up over its head then back down.

"Hold on, baby, I won't chu to save that first nut for me. Okay?" She glanced over at him smirking.

"I got chu, baby, I got chu." He hissed and licked his lips sensually.

Italia was about to roll up into the driveway of the house that was for rent when an explosion shook the streets like a Godzilla footstep, causing the BMW to swerve. She quickly gained control of her vehicle and peered over her shoulder. The door of a burning tattered house swung open and two Mexican men and a white woman came running out. From the latex gloves and the surgical masks they were wearing, Fear could tell that they had been doing something illegal. If he had to put his finger on it, he would have to say that they had been cooking methamphetamine and their homemade lab exploded.

"Oh my God, my baby, my baby's in the house!" the dirty blonde white woman screamed hysterically as one of the men held her back, trying to stop her from running back into the burning house.

"You can't, Martha, the place is an inferno," one of the Mexican men told her as he looked on at the burning house. Hearing the blaring sirens of fire trucks on their way, he looked to the other Mexican man and said, "Mano, we've gotta go! The policia is on the way, we don't want that static, hombre."

The Mexican man looked from his comrade to his white girlfriend.

"I'm sorry, baby," he told her with sorrowful eyes before darting off with his comrade. The white girl looked on in shock as her boyfriend left her to deal with her problem. She couldn't believe that he'd left her like that.

"Stop the car!" Fear ordered, looking from the burning house to Italia.

Urkkkkkkkkk!

The BMW came to a halt leaving black skid marks in the middle of the street.

"You gotta blanket or something?" he asked, holding the door halfway open.

"Yeah, in the trunk," Italia pressed the button that activated the trunk. Thunk!

Fear hopped out and ran to the rear of the Beemer, throwing the trunk open. He pulled out a thick plaid blanket and dashed over to the burning house. He grabbed the water hose and soaked the blanket.

"What floor is the baby on?" Fear called out to the white girl.

"The second floor. The master bedroom, down the hall to the left."

"Anyone else in the house?"

"There are two pit bulls."

"Are you thinking about going in there?" Italia approached.

"Yeah." Fear nodded, throwing the wet blanket around his shoulders.

"Alvin you've gotta be crazy!"

He looked her square in the eyes. "Fucking insane."

"Oh, thank you, thank you." the white girl held her hands together like she was praying.

"Alvin…" Italia grabbed his shoulder as he moved to head into the house, stopping him.

"Stop it, Italia. I'm going in there and I'm gonna do something right for once in my life," he stated sternly.

"You stubborn bastard." She cupped his face, kissing him quick and passionately. She pulled her head back but he grabbed her, kissing her a little longer. With that out of the way, he went charging into the flaming house like a superhero into the height of danger. As soon as Fear ran in across the threshold inside of the house, he began sweating instantly under the sweltering heat. The golden orange flames surrounding him, shining on his face and roaring like a den full of lions. He moved about swiftly narrowly avoiding the wreckage that fell from the ceiling, nearly crushing him. Setting his eyes on the staircase he moved forward, but not before being pounced on.

"Oooof!"

He fell to the floor with a blue silver, red nose pit bull on him, biting into his forearm as if it were a raw steak. The beast whipped its head back and forth trying to tear flesh from bone as it growled. Grrrrrr! Grrrrrr!

"Arghhhh!"

Fear grimaced, face wrinkling as he punched the animal as hard as he could.

Crack Crackk! Whrack!

He threw his fist with all of his might but his assault did nothing to thwart off the dog. Remembering the switch-blade that he kept stashed in his back pocket, he pulled it out and flicked the blade. He slammed the blade into the beast's eyeball drawing a howl of pain from it and causing it to release its powerful jaws from his forearm. He watched the pit as it scurried away running out of the house. Slowly, he scrambled to his feet. When he turned around he was face to face with another pit bull. Its head was tilted down and it was baring its fangs, its upper lip quivering as it growled angrily. This one was all white with brown, black striped patches.

Waa! Waa! Waa! Waa! Waa!

The wails of the baby drew his attention to the staircase which the hostile hound was guarding. He knew that he had to get to the baby fast for it may have been being burned. He could hear the faint screams of the mother just outside of the door. Fire fighters were racing back and forth across the lawn just outside the doorway. They strapped up with their equipment and drew white hoses so that they could drench the blazing house while others entered.

Grrrrrr!

Fear tilted his head and glared up at the beast baring his teeth just as it had.

"Alright, come on, cock sucka!"

The dog took off after him and he was right behind it. It leaped up into the air and he threw up his arm just as it showcased its saliva dripping fangs. The canines sank right into the young man's arm, causing him to drop his switchblade. He danced around the flaming living room with the dog, trying to tear his arm from out of his socket. His face tightened, pulling the skin at the center of it as he clenched his teeth. He hoisted the dog up and slammed its head against the doorway of the kitchen, all the while hearing the baby crying. The animal yelped and fell to the floor. Fear darted over to the staircase. With a couple of kicks, he was able to kick one of the white wooden rods loose. When the rod came loose he held it into an engulfed curtain until it caught fire. Hastily, he whipped around just in time to see the wild dog charging and leaping into the air, sharp teeth aimed at the throbbing vein in his neck.

Crackkkk!

The force of the wooden rod sent the dog slamming up against the wall. It fell on its feet but the young man was on him like strippers on trick ass niggaz. Grrrrr! The pit stared up at him with a bloody gash in its head. Crack! Crackk! Crackkk! Whack! The last swat left the animal dead with its tongue hanging out of its mouth. Fear's chest thumped like he had subwoofers installed inside of it. He breathed hard. His cheeks inflating and deflated as he held to the burning rod. Hearing the wails of the baby snapped him out of his zone and he tossed the rod aside. He went to recover his wet blanket but found that it had been swallowed by the fire. With not a second to waste, he made his way up the staircase with wreckage falling all around him. He moved from left to right dodging fiery chunks of the floor above. Hearing the ceiling shift, he looked up where he was on the staircase and saw it falling toward him. His eyes widen and his mouth formed an O. He ran and he leaped forth, both arms extended and hands ready to grab. The chunk of the ceiling blew out half of the staircase just as he reached the first half of it. He latched onto two of the wooden rods. His face was shiny with beads of sweat masking it due to the raging heat. The golden orange flames of the fire illuminated his entire form.

"Arghhhhhhhh!"

He belted out in excruciation. The wooden rods were hot and burned his palms. He held onto a rod with one hand while he looked at the other wincing. The flesh on the inside of his hand bubbled like soapy water. He looked over his shoulder down into the basement. It was being devoured by the vindictive fire. He was sure that if he fell that he'd be swallowed whole. Fighting back the pain, he grabbed a hold of the other rod and pulled himself up. He staggered up the steps and into the hall, looking at his hands and down the hall. He listened closely for the cries of the baby. Once he located the door, he went to turn the knob but saw that it was so hot that it was glowing like a charcoal. He stepped back and kicked it three times at the lock, busting it open like the mothafucking police.

Boom!

Froooosh!

The flames roared in his face and he held an arm over his brow, trying to peer into the bedroom. The doorway was lit but he could see a baby's crib and hear the infant's cries. Covering his face with his arms, he ran through the doorway and into the bedroom. He looked into the crib and thanked God that the little dude was all right. He scooped him up and held him to his chest. When he turned around the doorway had been completely swarmed by the fire. He whipped around and the bedroom window was masked by flames too. Seeing no other choice in the matter, he decided to drop his nuts and let them hang to the floor.

"Fuck it!" he said of the hazard before him.

Fear ran as far back to the end of the room as he could. Turning to the window, he held the baby as close to him as possible. He silently counted down in his head before he took off like a wide receiver, screaming at the top of his lungs. His eyes were squeezed closed tightly and his teeth were gritted as he went flying through the window, exploding the glass. Broken shards sliced up his arms, hands and face. He went hurling towards the front lawn with his arm and the side of his neck on fire. Pieces of glass were falling with him. The police, the fire fighters, Italia and the white girl were all staring up at him. He appeared to be falling towards the ground in slow motion with the shards moving along with him.

"Hooof!" Fear tucked and rolled on the lawn coming back upon his feet, still clutching the baby to his chest. A fire fighter rushed over spraying him with a fire extinguisher. The young man's eyelids peeled open and he looked up to the white girl. Her hands were cupped at her mouth and her crying eyes looked hopeful that he'd saved her child. He stood erect and limped forth, still holding the infant to his chest. He stopped before her and extended his arms. She took the baby and peeled the pale yellow blanket back that covered its face, it was okay. She whimpered and tears cascaded her face, she wrapped an arm around Fear and kissed him on the side of his face. He grimaced as her touch caused friction against his cuts and burns.

"Aww, thank you, thank you, thank you."

"You're…welcome," he grimaced.

The police took the baby from the woman and slapped cold metal bracelets on her skinny ass, ushering her away. Italia ran over and hugged Fear. He held her tight but fell slack, hitting the lawn on his side with his entire world spinning as if it was on spin-cycle.

"Did you see that shit, man?" a bystander spoke in amazement.

"Did I? He just came flying out of that window," a second bystander added.

"I've never seen anything like it before," a third one stated.

"He was extraordinary."

"He was spectacular."

"He was...he was...Fearless."

Those were the last words that young Alvin heard before he was swept away by the darkness.

Tranay Adams

CHAPTER THREE
2003
One night later

Fear's eyes fluttered open but his vision was out of focus. All he could see were blurred images and the sounds of a heart monitor at work amongst other medical machinery. When his vision was restored to its original 20/20, he saw Italia sitting to his left holding his hand. His lips twitched as he tried to form what was a crooked smile.

"Heyyy you," she beamed brightly, showcasing that enchanting smile of hers. She stood to her feet and caressed the side of his face.

"Hey, baby." He was just as happy to see her as she was to see him. Shit, he thought he'd died after that death defying stunt he'd pulled. After looking himself over, he saw that he was wearing an IV in his hand while his other arm was wrapped up in gauze; burgundy speckles showing from his wounds. His hands were also wrapped up from the burns he'd gotten from gripping those hot ass wooden rods on the staircase back at the burning house that was functioning as a meth lab.

"You are a hero." She grabbed the Los Angeles Times newspaper from off of the nightstand and passed it to him. He flipped it open and looked over the front page article: Youth saves baby from burning meth lab. Under the headline, there is a picture of him kneeling on the lawn clutching the baby to his chest while a fire fighter extinguishes the flames from his burning body. Fear looked above the heading of the paper, it was a day old.

"Hmmm." He handed her the newspaper back, unimpressed.

"That's it? That's all you have to say?" she asked surprised, tossing the newspaper back on the nightstand.

"I did what I did because I felt that it was the right thing to do," he spoke from the heart. "I wasn't looking for any praise or rewards afterwards, ya Griff me?"

"Well, rather you wanted them or not, you got 'em."

"Hey, what are ya gonna do?" he spat rhetorically, sitting up in bed and rubbing his throat, grimacing. He was parched, so he picked up the plastic cup and pitcher from off the nightstand.

"You know, your mother and father came up here to see you," she said looking over her French tipped nails, one hand at a time, admiring the design of them.

"Is that right?" he questioned, taking a sip from the cup.

"Yeah, about thirty five minutes ago," she reported, looking around the room. "Your father had to pry her from your bedside. You would have thought you were dying or something the way she performed."

"Just like ma to turn a cold into cancer." He slightly smirked, thinking about how his mother had always worried about him. She was always paranoid when he left the house. It didn't matter if he was going to school or to the East side to kick it with his cousins. She always thought of the worse that could happen. Although he complained, he was grateful to have someone in his life that gave a shit whether he lived or died.

My momma, my most favorite girl in the world, he shook his head thinking that his old lady was something else, placing the cup back down on the nightstand.

"I promised her that if you woke up tonight that I'd have you hit her up." She pressed the speed dial button and passed her cell off to Fear.

"Nah." He shook his head, "I'm not fucking with it right now, maybe later."

"Why?" an indention formed across her forehead.

"Pop, may answer and I ain't got shit to say to him, straight up."

"Never mind him. You needa call ya mother. She's worried sick about cha black ass."

"Nah, I'm good."

"Pretty please," she spoke with sad eyes and a pouty bottom lip.

"No." He gave her a dead serious look.

She angled her head and gave him sad eyes making her bottom lip quiver.

Fear closed his eyes and growled, arms folded across his chest.

"Me and my tender hearted ass." Exhaling, he took the cell from a smiling Italia who was pleased with his decision.

"Thank you, sweetie." She kissed her palm and blew him a kiss.

"Don't think that shit gon' keep on working. I ain't no simp."

As soon as he disconnected the call from talking with his mother, he heard a knock at the door. When he looked up, he found his paternal twin cousins, Malik and Wameek, entering his room. The young thug smiled as he was pleased with their presence.

"What's up with it, Blood?" Malik slapped hands with Fear and embraced him. He was the oldest of the pair by just five minutes. He was tall and slender, with a dusty brown complexion and features that made him look like a Haitian. The darker Simpson twin wore a thin goatee and his long thick hair in box braids. He was the calm to his younger sibling's storm.

"What's popping, family?"

"Ain't about shit, you know me and bruh bruh hadda come check on our loved one."

"Appreciate it, Big Dog."

"My nigga, Wa, what it two, baby?" he greeted his cousin with the same love he did his brother.

Wameek was a knucklehead with a body covered in muscles and tattoos. He rocked his hair in five big cornrows and wore a gold grill accented by diamonds. He lived for the drama and often found ways to create it out of pure boredom. The mothafucka was something wicked. If the devil really did walk amongst the living, it had to be as him. Once he got started tearing shit up, the only one that could stop him was his twin. That was one cat that he admired and respected to the utmost. Wameek was a vicious ass Rottweiler and his oldest brother was definitely the nigga holding his leash.

"What's brackin', Duse Owe?" he embraced him. While doing so he looked over his shoulder and spotted Italia who rolled her eyes and looked her nails over again. He'd tried her for the pussy on several occasions and each time she'd shot him down. Never mind the fact that he knew that she and his cousin had an unofficial thing going. He didn't give a fuck because he was a sleaze bag like that. Wameek was the kind of cat that would push up on his best friend's baby's momma. See, to him there wasn't a bitch that wasn't off limits. That was unless she belonged to his big brother, of course.

"'Sup 'Talia?" Wameek threw his head back.

"What's up, Wameek?" Italia blew hot air, annoyed.

Malik and Wameek pulled up chairs to their cousin's hospital bed.

"How you been, G?" Malik leaned back as his brother reached across him to grab the orange from off the nightstand. As soon as he sat down, he began peeling the fruit.

"Alright, in this bitch laid up," Fear answered. "Where y'all two niggaz coming from?"

"The hood, we were at that nigga Jeff's tattoo shop gettin' blasted up."

"For real? What y'all get?" he asked curiously.

"Our sister's face," Wameek spoke up. He stood to his feet and held up his Atlanta Falcon's jersey. His stomach had old stab wounds and keloids from gunshots. On his right peck was an exact replica of his sister's face. Rest in peace Christine Simpson along with her birth and death date was below it. When he let his jersey fall back over his stomach, his brother showcased the same tattoo on him, but his was on his ribcage.

Malik and Wameek were the children of Deon Simpson and Nicole Wheaton; a two bit pimp and his bottom bitch. One night they were abducted from the hoe stroll. Only to be found days later, dismembered in a dumpster just outside of a nightclub. Rumor had it, that they'd been butchered on the account of Nicole stealing jewelry and money from a Russian mafia associate she'd sexed a few days prior. The twins went to stay with their older sister on the East Side of Los Angeles in a poverty stricken section called the Low Bottoms. Although the murders brought both devastation and grief to the Simpson family, it also left the nineteen year old sister, Christine, to raise her twin brothers alone. She may have gotten some financial assistance from her relatives, but in the end it just wasn't enough. Needless to say, she had to do what she had to in order to keep a roof over their heads. Eventually Christine became a victim of her circumstances and turned to heroin to escape her harsh reality. Due to her habit she neglected her responsibilities as her siblings' guardian and they were taken away from her and placed into a foster home. She found herself dead broke and living on the streets; sleeping with every Tom, Dick and Harry to keep the monkey off of her back. When it had gotten to the point that niggaz wasn't trying to fuck with her to pacify her fix, she resorted to stealing from the dealers from around her way. She'd gotten away without incident twice, but the third time wasn't a charm. When the trap boy went to serve a dope fiend this time, he had his homeboy hiding in the recesses of the alley. When Christine went to try for the stash, the homeboy snuck up behind her and cracked her across the back of the head with a 2 x 4. When she finally came to, she was deep inside of the bowels of an abandoned tenement gagged and bound to an iron chair. The trap boy had filled a syringe with battery acid and injected it into her vein. It took the police three weeks to find her body. The acid had eaten away her eyeballs and left blood running from every hole in her face. Her hands and feet had been gnawed down to the bone by rodents.

Malik and Wameek caught up with the trap boy and his homeboy six months later. They chained them up to a rusty pipe inside of the same tenement that their sister's corpse was found in. Armed with metal baseball bats, they beat the men within an inch of their lives before delivering the Death Blows to the backs of their craniums. When the bodies were discovered the media charged it as a gangland style execution, but the hood knew better than that. There were whispers of why the men were murdered and who had done the deed, but that knowledge was withheld from the public because the community sympathized with The Simpson family. Not to mention the ancient old creedal that was still upheld then: no snitching.

"So, uh, when they lettin' you outta here, my nigga?" Malik sat back in his chair.

"He's going to stay one more day, so the doctor can run some more tests and make sure he's alright."

Malik looked to Fear and he gave him a nod.

"Listen, I've got something I wanna talk to you about."

"What's that?" he asked, eyes narrowing. When he saw his oldest cousin cut his eyes at Italia, he instantly picked up on what he was getting at. Knowing this, he gave him a nod and looked to his lady.

"Talia, give us a minute," Fear told her.

"Okay." She nodded and disappeared through the doorway.

"What's up?" Fear turned back around to Malik.

He looked around to make sure that no one was listening to what he had to say, before beginning.

"Cocaine," he spoke in a hushed tone.

"That ain't nothing new, we've been fucking with crack."

"Nah, nah, nah," he shook his head, "you not hearin' me, baby boy. Me and bruh bruh," he motioned his finger between he and Wameek, "got the hook up on a plug that's got some of the sweetest powder on the market and right now we tryna get our own White House, ya Griff me?"

"I follow you." He nodded. "So what chu working with? Consignment?"

"Consignment?" Malik's face balled up as he laughed, tapping his brother. "You hear this nigga, Blood? Talkin' 'bout owin' niggaz for some work? Come on now, we betta then that. Today is a new day, fam."

"What chu mean?" He frowned.

"I gotta check, homie, I'm finna load up on them pies."

Fear sat up in bed and said, "Fuck you getta check from?"

"Don't worry about all of that," he told him. "I jus needa know my lil' relative is still ridin' with his bloodline."

"Always." They slapped hands and pounded the Blood B gang sign against their chests.

"Good. 'Cause we meetin' up with this nigga tomorrow."

"Yeah, so be ready," Wameek added.

"Yo," Malik turned around in his chair, anger etched across his face. "Why don't chu get the fuck from outta here? You always got some extra bullshit to throw up in the mix."

Wameek twisted his lips and shook his head, rolling his eyes. "And what the fuck you rollin' ya goddamn eyes like a lil' ol' bitch for?" he shot to his feet, clenching his fists and mad dogging his younger brother.

Wameek shot to his feet with his hands up, looking afraid. He wasn't scared of anybody in the world, but his big brother put the fear of Christ in him.

"Bro, I didn't mean nothin' by it, I swear!"

"Get outta here!" he pointed at the door. When his sibling turned to walk away, he kicked him in the ass. "Get the fuck up from outta here, hoe ass nigga!" he staggered forward and almost fell, but he kept his monkey ass on out of that door.

Malik sat back down in the chair and straightened the collar of his jacket. "Sorry about that. My bro may be a pain in the ass, but chu can always count on him in a jam."

"Amen to that." Fear nodded his agreement.

CHAPTER FOUR
2003
The next day

"I was finally able to track your acquaintance down," Gustavo spoke from behind his desk to Black Jesus who was on the projection's screen. He clipped the end of the Cuban cigar in his mouth and his maid lit it. He took a couple of puffs and unleashed smoke. "Broomhilda, see to it that Maldonado gets a glass of homemade lemonade, please."

"Yes, Mr. Sanchez."

"Oh, and I have three guests that will be here shortly to see me."

"Yes, sir." The maid nodded and closed the door on her way out.

"Is that so?" Black Jesus asked. He was a strikingly attractive man of a mahogany hue. His long curly hair made him resemble God's son. At first glance, one would mistake this powerful figure as an African American male, but his facial features were mostly those of a Latino.

"Uh huh, I told you my people would get right on it. It's been ten years since that night but the son of a bitch hasn't aged a bit." Gustavo grasped a portrait of a pretty teenage girl with long straight, brunette hair. He smiled affectionately at her as his thumb caressed the glass where her face was. This was his daughter. She'd committed suicide some time ago. Feeling moisture in his eyes and an aching in his heart, he sat the portrait face down.

Thinking about what had happened that night caused Black Jesus' forehead to deepened with lines. He gritted and clenched his fists so tight that his knuckles bulged in his hands.

Black Jesus was one of the biggest cocaine suppliers to the United States. His cartel moved over one hundred tons of cocaine a month. For years he had been under the watchful eyes of the D.E.A but they could never make anything stick. The District Attorney, while on lunch with a colleague, joked that they should start calling the pretty boy drug lord Slick the Spic. When asked why, he replied "Because he's as slippery as a snake. Somehow the son of a bitch always manages to slip right between my fingers. He's just too goddamn slick."

One night, without probable cause, the police pulled Black Jesus over. They told him he was swerving in and out of lanes and they believed that he was drunk, but that was all bullshit. They knew exactly who he was. His face was plastered on every news paper in the city and his trial was covered by every known news channel.

When asked to step out of his vehicle, the drug lord refused and locked the doors. He looked around and two more police cars had pulled up. He was just about to place a call to his lawyer when Police Sergeant Daniel O'Connor whacked the driver side window with his nightstick until the glass shattered. He and another cop pulled Black Jesus from the window and let him drop to the street. The drug lord tried to put up a fight but he was out numbered six to one.

Leaving the other cops to beat up the detainee, the sergeant and his men destroyed Black Jesus' vehicle looking for drugs. When they were done having their way with the car, it looked like the chop shop had gotten a hold of it. Pissed off that they didn't find any narcotics, the two of them gave the other officers a break from beating the Spanish Nino Brown's ass, and went to work on him themselves. Dragging the drug lord into the nearby woods, they beat him until his spine fractured, leaving him crippled from the waist down. Black Jesus was in so much pain that he wished the crooked bastards would just shoot him in the head and put him out of his misery.

O'Connor watched as his men took turns pissing on the broken man. The pale face, blue eyed devils laughed and high fived each other after they were done. Black Jesus had suffered a great deal, but the sergeant felt that it wasn't enough. He withdrew his nightstick and lubed it up with his own saliva. He pulled the drug lord's pants down around his ankles and ass fucked him with the cold nightstick. Being paralyzed from the waist down, Black Jesus couldn't feel a thing, but he knew something wasn't right. He was being violated and stripped of his manhood.

When O'Connor pulled his nightstick from Black Jesus' rectum, it was stained with blood and feces. He wiped the steel rod on his pants and returned it to its holster. He then spat on homeboy and he and his men left. Black Jesus wasn't found until the next morning; an elderly man taking his 6 A.M jog discovered him and called the police. When he woke up in the hospital, he was so traumatized and embarrassed about the whole ordeal that he made the doctor and nurses promise not to release any information to his family about his torn rectum. His loved ones were only to know that he had been beaten and left paralyzed. If it were to ever get out that he had been violated, his reputation would be torn to shreds. The only people to know was his brother, Bullet and Gustavo, his truest friend.

Black Jesus took a deep breath and calmed himself down. His shoulders dropped and he unclenched his fists, breathing hard. Finally, he closed and peeled open his eyelids. Licking his lips, he stated coolly, "When it's done, you be sure to get my confirmation."

"You have my word." He gave him a firm look. He knew what those bastards had done to his dear friend and he wanted them all dead. Over the years they picked them off one by one, using different cats to take on the hits then murdering them once the job was done. Now they had one more to take care of: Sergeant Daniel O'Connor. One his ass was resting with the maggots and the worms, Black Jesus would finally have his revenge.

"Who are you using?"

"A couple of guys eager to make their bones," he informed him. "Don't worry. They aren't connected to me, I know that's the way you want it."

"Exactly…thank you."

"Don't mention it." He gave him a nod and killed the projection screen. A knock at the door brought his attention around.

"Malik is here to see you, sir."

He took the cigar out of his mouth and said, "I'll be right out."

Gustavo pulled open his desk drawer and removed his binoculars, taking a photograph as well. He stole a glance through the window of his study at something in the lake in his backyard. He stood there for a moment before heading out of the door.

***

Malik pulled up in front of Gustavo's estate and jumped out, slamming the door shut behind him. Wameek and Fear jumped out right after him on his heels. Walking up, they all gazed up at the mansion which looked like a baby castle. Taking their eyes off of the home, they took in the rest of their surroundings. The lawn was a rich green and was well manicured. They could tell that whoever the South American cocaine distributor had hired to be his gardener had done a good job maintaining its upkeep. Ironically at the moment, a Mexican man in a sun hat and sweat stained wife beater drove around in a motorized lawnmower, cutting the grass. A maid came out the front doors of the mansion with a tray carrying a pitcher of homemade lemonade and an empty glass. The Mexican man took off his hat and patted the beads of sweat from his forehead with a handkerchief. He smacked the hat back upon his head and took the glass of lemonade, guzzling it until every last drop was gone.

"Ahhhh." He sat the glass on the tray and went on about his business, making a U-turn in his lawnmower. The threesome looked away from the gardener and focused back on the land. Just outside the double doors of the mansion was a fifteen foot statue of the man that they'd come to see: Gustavo. The bushes and trees were trimmed and sculpted so well that they made the place look like it came straight off the cover of Home & Garden magazine. The kingpin's crib was all of that and then some. It deserved its own episode of MTV cribs.

"Are you here to see Mr. Sanchez?" the maid spoke, holding the tray on both ends.

"Yeah," Malik nodded.

"Follow me please." She smiled, leading the way. She pulled out a cell phone and pressed a button that dialed someone up with the quickness. The person on the other side of phone answered immediately. While she rattled off some shit in a thick Spanish accent, the fellas zeroed in on the Tech Nine on her hip. They frowned and exchanged glances. Although the petite woman seemed timid and harmless, it became obvious that she was with the shit if drama was ever brought to the home front.

As soon as the maid opened the doors and the cousins crossed the threshold, they were in awe. Wow was plastered across their faces as they took in the full scope of the foyer. An enormous chandelier hung from the ceiling with fiery yellow lighting that illuminated everything surrounding it. The Italian imported tiled floors were so shiny that they could see their reflections in it. Fear looked down at his feet and was impressed with the clarity of his appearance. He was so mesmerized that he didn't snap out of it until he heard the maid speak again.

"Mr. Sanchez will be right with you gentlemen." She sauntered off with Wameek's eyes lingering on her ass. He licked his lips and rubbed his hands together mischievously, like he had some nasty things in mind to do to her. His big brother's brows wrinkled and he nudged him, stealing his attention. He shot him a look that he read as Leave that shit at the door, nigga. In hushed tones, the siblings argued back and forth until they heard a husky voice, that straightened them both right up. When they looked up, they saw Gustavo and his bodyguard, Lethal, approaching.

"Malik." Gustavo took the cigar from his thin lips and switched hands with it. He shook the young nigga'z hand, maintaining eye contact with him. Lethal wore a stone face as he gave a slight nod to the cousins as a collective. They returned the gesture.

"What's up, G?" He shook his hand holding one hand over his own.

"Who are these gentlemen?" He looked to Wameek and Fear.

"My baby bro and my lil' blood cousin," he introduced them with a sway of his hand. Gustavo greeted them with a nod and a firm handshake.

"Come along." He motioned for them to follow him and Lethal as they turned and headed down the hallway. Malik walked beside him while Fear and Wameek brought up their rear. The young nigga'z eyes studied the portraits aligning the wall. Most of them were of whom he assessed were the kingpin's family and friends. When he spotted the largest portrait at the center of the corridor, he slowed his roll and looked closely. In the picture there were Gustavo and a host of made men. They were all in golfing gear holding golf clubs and cigars pinched between their fingers. At the center of the jovial men and one person behind them was a tall, strapping young man with a thin mustache. Fear narrowed his eyes, stuck his head out and massaged his chin as he tried to recall who the youngster was. When the name came across his mental, he snapped his fingers and a cracked a grin.

"That's who that is."

"Psssss!" A voice called for his attention. When he looked up, he saw a scowling Wameek waving him over so that they could catch up with the other men. Fear jogged up the hallway to rejoin them. The foursome stepped out into the backyard which was long and vast, giving way to a lake. Gustavo stood facing the body of water and smoking his cigar, watching something off into the distance. Sticking one hand into the pocket of his slacks while the other held his overgrown cigarette, he turned back around to face the cousins who were taking in the full scope of their surroundings.

"Tell me, Malik, how much product do you plan to take off of my hands? 'Cause I've gotta tell you, I don't fuck with short money. I'd be looking for you to cop at least thirty kilos at a time at fifteen grand a piece." He pointed at him with the hand that he held his cigar with. "I'm giving you such a sweet deal for what chu did for me. I feel it's only right that I pay my debts. That's what men of our caliber do, I'm sure you would agree."

"I most definitely do." He nodded his agreement. "And don't worry about it, I got that easy."

"Do I have your word?" Their eyes locked with intensity.

"On the graves of my parents." He held up his hand.

"Good enough." The drug lord looped the binoculars from around his neck and waved him over. "Come here. I'd like to show you something." Malik stepped forth and he passed him the binoculars. He stood beside him, pointing out into the water. He looked to him then to the lake. "You see him?"

Wameek and Fear looked further out into the water, hands above their brows for a closer look.

"Yeah," Malik replied, seeing through the binoculars. Lethal stood behind a man that was on his knees in a boat begging and pleading for his life. Creases went across the cousins' foreheads as they didn't know what the drug lord's purpose was for showing them this.

"That's my nephew Caesar down on his knees," Gustavo announced. "I caught him stealing from me, can you believe it?" He took the time to take a draw from his cigar.

"It's a cold world," Fear proclaimed. "You've gotta keep your eyes on your family and your enemies."

"Indeed," Gustavo looked over his shoulder at the short killer then focused on the lake, making eye contact with Lethal. He extended his hand with his thumb up and then quickly turned it down. Bop! The gunshot echoed and everyone flinched except Fear. The youngest Simpson wore a solemn expression as he watched the killer stand over his victim and finish the job. Bop! Bop! Bop! Bop! All in his mothafucking top.

Murder wasn't anything new to Fear. It was ground that he'd already covered and he was sure that he'd most likely do it again. Malik took the binoculars from his eyes and passed them back to Gustavo. The message was clear: If I did this to my own blood, imagine what I'd do to you if you were to ever try to fuck me.

"You want your keys at ten grand a piece? Fine, but you're gonna earn it."

Malik's forehead deepened with lines. "Wait a minute. I thought that thing that I did for you got us that."

"I'm afraid not. What chu did got chu an introduction."
He told him flat out. "This mission gets you the price on
the merchandise you desire." He cracked a wicked smile,
looking like the Devil.

***

Gustavo and his date had just emerged from out of
Raphael's, an Italian restaurant out in Hollywood. The drug
lord stuck a cigar into his mouth and cupped his hand
around it, roasting it with a flame until smoke gave. He
took a couple of draws as his younger, drunken female
companion fondled on him. Her hand took a tour down his
belly, grasping his meat through his slacks. She gently bit
on his earlobe and pulled on it, before sucking on it. Her
hot breath felt good on his neck and moistened it even.

"Where the fuck is Eduardo with the limousine?" He
frowned, looking up and down the street for the vehicle he
was chauffeured there in. It was like he didn't even notice
he had a very attractive young lady sex playing him.

Feeling neglected seeing as how he wasn't paying her
any attention, she turned him to face her by his chin and
locked eyes with him. She slipped her tongue between his
lips and kissed him hard and sensually. When she pulled
back, she wiped the excess spit from the corner of his
mouth as well as hers.

"I just want cho big brown ass to know one thing, Mr.
Man." She softly bit and sucked on his neck, making him
grow hard in his slacks groping him.

"Oh...oh, yeah? Well...well, what's that?" His eyes
rolled up to their whites and he dropped the burning cigar
at his black leather Mauri shoe.

"I'm going to suck the skin off of your big. Brown.
Dick," she whispered into his ear, warming and moistening
it. Seeing the limo that had drove them there, she looked
alive and grabbed his meaty hand.

"There's our ride, we'll finish this once were inside." She stepped to the curb excitedly, ready to give her sponsor the blow job of his life. That's when it happened. A hoodlum in a dingy T-shirt and jeans torn at the knees ran past her, yanking her gold necklace from her neck. "Ughh! Haa!" she gasped and her eyes went wide as she smacked a hand over her chest where her necklace used to be. She and Gustavo's eyes followed the thief as he hauled ass down the sidewalk, clutching her necklace in his hand.

Vroooooooooooom!

A sexy red Kawasaki Ninja blew past them, ruffling their hair and clothing. The motorcyclist was wearing a sleek helmet and matching leather jacket. Bike squealing with its front wheel up in the air as he was en route toward the hoodlum that had snatched the drug lord's woman's necklace. The hood was running as hard and as fast as he could, occasionally glancing over his shoulder. "Oh shit!" he breathed hard, seeing the Ninja on his ass. His eyes bugged and the moisture dried from his mouth. Homeboy was scared out of his mind. Schick! The motorcyclist snatched the baseball bat from where it was sheathed on his ride, spinning it around in his gloved hand and grasping it.

The gloved hand came up and above the motorcyclist's head and swung it with all of his strength. The baseball bat broke in half sending splinters and debris every which way. The thief grimaced and rolled like tumble weed, losing the necklace and lying flat out on the corner. He groaned in pain. The hurt he felt caused his eyes to moisten and he squared his jaws. Inching his head from off of the sidewalk, he saw his attacker toss the broken half of the bat aside and do a donut in the middle of the street, en route in his direction. The hood scrambled to his feet hastily still feeling the aching in his back. He hurried along as fast as he could, trying to make it into a nearby alley. The man on the Ninja leaned to the side and snatched up the necklace, depositing it into his jacket's pocket. He stopped at the mouth of the alley watching the thief get along as best as he could, holding his back and constantly peering over his shoulder. Right after, he zipped right back up the block and stopped before the drug lord and his trophy piece, flipping up the black tinted visor. It was Malik.

He pulled the necklace free from his jacket's pocket and passed it off to the lady. She thanked him, opened her handbag, and dropped it inside of it. Gustavo stepped forth and outstretched his hand, giving him a smirk.

"Thanks." He nodded and pulled a folded knot of hundred dollar bills from his pocket, removing the gold money clip. "Here, let me give you a little something for your trouble."

"Nah, nah, I couldn't take yo' money, fam." Malik held up a hand for him to stop.

"You sure?" He raised an eyebrow and about five Benjamin Franklins, ready to hand over the bills if he was willing to take them.

"I'm good."

He slipped the money clip back on the bills and slid them back inside of his pocket.

"Okay. If you won't take my money, then what will you take then?" He smacked his hands against one another and rubbed them together.

"Your friendship." He outstretched his gloved hand. The drug lord stared at it for a time allowing it to linger before he eventually shook it firmly.

Malik and Gustavo chopped it up for a time before he was given his card. They shook hands again before departing. The drug lord and his lady were whisked away by a luxurious limousine while the hero left on his bike. He pulled into a McDonald's parking lot beside a red Jeep Cherokee truck where Wameek was playing the driver side blowing that Loud, the sounds of Styles P's I Get High rattling the SUV's black tinted windows and trunk. When he saw his older brother, he let down the window and a fog escaped into the air, eventually disappearing.

"What's up, Blood? We good?" He threw his head back as he blew out smoke.

"A1." He smiled and rubbed his gloved hands together greedily. "Where's Tyrone at so I can bless 'em?"

The back window descended and revealed, Tyrone, the hood he'd struck over the back with a baseball bat. He was wincing and rubbing the lower half of his back.

"Got damn, nigga, you almost broke my back. Sssssss, shit!" The crack head complained, bending backwards.

"My fault, Blood, I had to make it look good." He tried to explain. "But don't trip, 'cause I'ma hook you up."

Malik and Wameek did their homework on Gustavo. They knew that he was supplying the streets with some of the best cocaine money could buy. This was why they had used crack head Tyrone to stage the entire necklace snatching thing. They figured that if they got into his good graces that he was sure to give them a decent price on some bricks.

Malik took a cautious look around to make sure that no one was watching what he about to do. Figuring that he was in the clear, he pulled out four off white crack rocks and passed them to the junkie. Next, he pulled out a few folded dead white men and peeling a couple off, passing them to him through the window. Tyrone's eyes became as big as saucers and his jaw dropped, exposing the wide gaps between his beige teeth.

"Good lookin' out, Boss Dawg." He stuffed his reward into his pocket and hopped out. Malik patted him on his back as he took off, disappearing into the night.

"We on?" Wameek asked Malik as he threw his leg over the seat of his Ninja.

"Oh yeah, we on." He answered, sliding his helmet on his head.

"A hunnit bucks to the twin that makes it home first."

Malik kicked up his kickstand with his boot heel and revved up his motorcycle. Looking to his younger brother, he nodded and accepted his challenge. He sped out of the McDonald's parking lot with his sibling following closely behind.

Malik took a deep breath and said, "Alright, what a nigga gotta do?"

"I thought you'd never ask. Tell me, have you ever killed someone before?"

Malik pointed to the red tattoo tears going down the right side of his face.

With that gesture, Gustavo pulled a photograph from inside of his suit and handed it to him. The young hustler stared at the photo inquisitively. It was of a white Irish American cop receiving an award of some sort. The Irishman had a thin mustache and an athletic physique. While Malik looked over the photo, the drug lord watched him curiously taking pulls from his cigar.

"I take it you want us to waste this cat?" Malik looked up from the photograph.

He nodded yes. "Is there a problem?"

"Yeah, this mothafucka is One Time." He looked at him like You can't be serious.

"Yes, he's a cop, and so what. Cops aren't anything but people with guns. And I have plenty of those in my employ." He reached for the photograph saying, "Look, I can see you're not up for this so…"

"Never mind my relative," Fear interjected. "If all we have to do is led some pig to slaughter to get a 15k ticket price, then so be it. Shit, I'd sneak my black ass into Jerusalem and lay down Jesus and his twelve apostles if it meant I could get work for fifteen a key. I'd be a mothafucking fool not to." He rubbed his hands together greedily as he bit down on his bottom lip.

The price on Gustavo's cocaine was so cheap because he got it straight off of the boat for five grand a key. He stood to make ten grand off of each brick so the way he saw it he was winning anyway.

"I like the way you think." Gustavo smiled.

Fear took the photo from Malik. He looked at the man presented in it and then he turned it over and read the address on the back of it. "Tomorrow you'll be having smothered pork chops for dinner."

"Hold on," Malik started, holding his hand against Fear's chest. "Why do you want this cat's momma in a black dress so bad?" he asked with a Don't give me any bullshit either expression.

"My friend, some questions are better left unanswered."

Malik nodded his understanding.

Gustavo took the binoculars away from him just as the maid stepped out the backdoor. He didn't even bother to turn around. His focus was on the boat as Lethal stuck Caesar in a body bag and chained him to boulders.

Wameek, Fear and Malik stared up ahead watching the entire procedure taking place.

"Make no mistake, killing a cop; crooked or otherwise, can get you the gas chamber. So if you're caught …"

"We already know," Malik cut him short. "You don't even have to stress that."

"I would hope so." Gustavo took a pull of his cigar. "Broomhilda, will you see these three gentlemen out?"

***

The Simpsons made their way down the steps of Gustavo's mansion heading for the car.

"So what's the deal?" Fear asked, slamming the door shut as he hopped into the backseat.

"The deal is you're taking 'em out." Malik relayed as if it weren't a big deal.

The backseat grew quiet as he settled back, head slumped thinking with his hands resting inside the pockets of his red hoodie. Once he was done tossing his decision back and forth inside of his head; he looked up and said, "Alright, I'll do it. I'll take 'em out."

"That's what I'm talking about." Malik smiled with joy while applauding,"I knew my relative wouldn't let us down."

Wameek turned around, looking into the backseat he said, "You sure you wanna go through with rocking this pig to sleep? I mean, if you're scared we could..."

"Blood, don't chu ever in your mothafucking life bring that scared shit to me!" he roared, "Fuck you think they call me Fearless for, huh?"

"My fault, Mr. Get Bad," Wameek cracked a gold tooth smile, holding his hands up, "I'm just saying, I don't wanna put any pressure on you is all."

"The pressure ain't gon' be too much on 'em 'cause you going to watch his back," Malik interjected.

Wameek's neck coiled and he frowned. "How you figure?"

Malik scowled and said, "'Cause I said so, bitch!"

Slap!

The younger brother's head snapped forward and he looked to his big brother rubbing the back of it.

"Ouch!"

"Yo' ass going, you hear? And I don't wanna hear shit about it."

"Alright, man, damn." He winced.

Fear stared up front watching everything unfold. He was taken by surprise when he saw Malik slap his brother upside the head.

"And there you have it, my young nigga." Malik stole a glance at him through the rearview mirror, smiling like he just didn't slap his twin brother. "You got cho people rollin' witchu so that should ease yo' worries."

"Ain't no worries, family," Fear rubbed his hands together in anticipation for the mission. "This nigga'z number is up and I'm gonna be the one to call it."

"You're getting down for the movement my nigga, respect." He nodded as he held his gaze through the rearview mirror.

"Yep." Fear threw his hood over his head. Leaning back, he shut his eyes and thought about the hit he was supposed to carry out. Before long he'd fallen asleep and Malik was watching him through the rearview mirror. Hmmph, he thought to himself. He couldn't see how his cousin could sleep like a baby knowing that he'd be killing a cop in the next couple of hours. If he only knew that his relative was like his name stated, Fearless.

CHAPTER FIVE
That night

Fear and Wameek sat in a Burger King parking lot across the street from where their intended mark was stationed. 2pac's Bomb First flowed softly from the speakers of the red Jeep Cherokee they were inside. They shared a Premo, a cocaine laced blunt between them, waiting for their man to exit the shopping center.

"Damn, Blood, this Kush is off the chain," Fear exclaimed behind glassy, red webbed eyes. "I've never fucked with any raw before, but this shit got my face going numb and shit. Is cocaine supposed to do that?" he asked Wameek, who was beside him in the passenger seat taking pulls of the laced blunt.

"Hell naw!" Wameek said, holding the smoke in his lungs. "This shit ain't pose to do that."

Fear looked at Wameek like a snake had sunken its fang into the tip of his penis. "Ah, shit, man! What the fuck that Spanish nigga done gave us?" He panicked, feeling his face as if he had just discovered he had one.

Wameek doubled over laughing. He laughed so hard that he began to tear. His little cousin was tripping hard off of the premo joint. He had seen many virgins of the laced joint react the same way as he did their first time trying it; minus the numbness of face thing. All that meant was Black Jesus had the best cocaine on the market and he was the nigga to fuck with.

"Nah, Blood, I'm serious!" Fear exclaimed. "I can't feel my shit!" He looked into the rearview mirror as he felt around his face. "Blood, you gone have to take me to the hospital, I think that mothafucka done poisoned me."

Wameek laughed even harder. "Nigga, chill the fuck out," he said. "You're straight. You 'pose to be numb like that. That means the yay we laced this bleezy with is off the hook. Sheiiitt, if Black Jesus' work is this good"-he looked at the Premo joint-"then he's definitely the spic we need to be fucking with. That's for damn sure." He hit the Premo and then blew smoke.

"Man, I'm not ever fucking with that bullshit again," he claimed, feeling around his face. "From now on, it's nothing but good old weed for me. Y'all can have the rest of that shit out here."

"Fucking rookie," Wameek chuckled and rolled down the window, flicking the roach out.

"Aye, that's them!" Fear nodded to the windshield at a car, grabbing his ski-mask.

"Where?" Wameek asked, snaking his neck as he looked through the windshield.

"Right there!" Fear pointed at the windshield to a gray Volvo station wagon making its way out of the shopping center across the street.

Fear pulled his ski-mask over his face, with Wameek following suit he resurrected the Jeep Cherokee and then slowly coasted out of the Burger King parking lot.

"Alright, blood, pulled to the light," Wameek said, after observing the Volvo stopping at a red traffic light. "Swing this bitch right out in front of him and we gone jump out on him."

Wameek reached into the backseat and grabbed two weapons: an Ak-47 and an Uzi .9mm. He kept the Ak-47 for himself and gave Fear the Uzi .9mm.

Meanwhile

Police Sergeant Daniel O'Connor and his family had just pulled out of the shopping center in their charcoal gray Volvo station wagon. The married couple and their children had just finished grocery shopping at the Food4Less Supermarket on Imperial and Western Avenue. Their identical twin sons, Kyle and Lyle, were in the backseat playing their Nintendo DSs'. Their mother, Carol, sat up front with their father, who was behind the wheel eating a caramel Drumstick ice cream.

O'Connor was a six foot Irishman in good shape for his age. He possessed radiant blue eyes, a handle bar mustache and rough, pale skin. He had craters in both of his cheeks. Whereas his family knew the kind, gentle and honorable Daniel, the streets knew the coldhearted, reckless and crooked as a barrel of snakes, Sergeant Daniel O'Connor. He had a reputation and a ruthlessness that matched some of the most infamous gangsters of Southern, California. After his demise, he'd surely be remembered as a legend amongst his peers and street niggaz, alike.

Pulling up to a red light, the fifty year old law enforcement veteran looked over to his wife of twenty odd years and found her staring out of the passenger side window.

"Wanna bite?" He asked, holding his Drumstick near her lips.

Carol turned around. She looked to the Drumstick and then to her husband. She smiled and then took a bite out of the coned ice cream.

"This is good," She said as she licked her lips.

O'Connor saw some vanilla ice cream trickle from the corner of his wife's mouth. He swept it off with his finger and sucked it off. Carol smiled and he smiled back. They then locked lips like high school sweethearts. Twenty three long years and they were still in love.

"Dad, Dad!" The twins shouted from the back seat in unison.

"What?" O'Connor asked annoyed, looking over his shoulder into the backseat.

"The light is green." Lyle answered, pointing to the windshield at the stop light. He was the youngest of the pair, entering this hectic world three minutes after his older brother, Kyle.

"We'll wrap this up later," O'Connor told his wife with a seductive look.

"You can count on it, tiger," she retorted, returning the seductive look.

When O'Connor turned his attention back onto the street, he was blinded by the bright headlights of an oncoming vehicle. The vehicle with the bright headlights swung out in front of the family's station wagon. The doors of the Ford Explorer swung open and two masked men jumped out. The first masked man was clutching an Uzi while the other gripped an AK-47.

The masked man clutching the Uzi paused in front of the driver side of the Volvo and held back the trigger of his machine gun. O'Connor managed to clear his Glock .23 halfway from its holster before his chest exploded in a mass of blood and gore. The sergeant slid over towards the passenger seat, his face twisted in agony. The twins went frantic, screaming and crying for their father. They unbuckled their safety belts and climbed half way over the seat to tend to their dying father.

"Carol, take the gun...protect the kids," O'Connor croaked his last words as he handed his gun to his wife.

"Oh my God, Daniel, Daniel!" she screamed terrified, hands trembling uncontrollably having seen her husband with his chest looking like a busted can of Sloppy Joe.

"Daddy! Daddy!" the boys whined from the backseat.

Carol was scared as hell, but she knew she had to give it her all and fight for the lives of her children, and her own as well. She wiped the tears from her face with the back of her shirt's sleeve, and took her husband's Glock into her hands. Just as she turned to open fire on the approaching masked man with the Ak-47, the windshield exploded into glass shards. The broken glass sprayed into her face, slicing it up. Her body jerked violently as the missile shaped bullets slammed into her chest and exited out of the back of the front passenger seat, narrowly missing her first born. She slid against the door panel and blood flowed over her chin as she stared out of lifeless eyes. She was dead.

The masked man with the Uzi sat his weapon on the hood of the Volvo and unsheathed his machete. The twins sobbed harder and louder as he reached inside and pulled their father's head out of the driver side window, lying his neck on the window seal.

"Daddy," Kyle screamed for his father, but he was long dead. His eyes were rolled to their whites and his plaid shirt was stained burgundy. He wasn't about to feel what was to happen next.

Snikttt!

The nigga that gave the sergeant the business drew his machete from where it was sheathed on his hip. Holding his head down by his hair, he swung the blade down with all of his might. Swhack! Swhack! The sharp metal nearly severed his head completely but it was still hanging on by a stubborn piece of his neck. Gritting, the masked gunman worked his head back and forth until it came loose. "Ugh." He staggered back a little but regained his equilibrium, sheathing his machete. He opened the sack on his waistline and deposited the severed head inside of it, pulling it closed with its drawstrings. Afterwards, he grabbed his Uzi off the hood of the station wagon and fled back to the Ford Explorer, sliding back in behind the wheel.

"Come on, man! Let's go!" He yelled out to his partner in crime, slamming the driver side door shut.

The masked man with the Ak-47 had opened the passenger door and begun removing the jewelry from the husband and wife's dead persons. He stuffed the jewelry into his jacket's pocket and then stuck his head out of the car, yelling back, "Here I come, Blood. Hold it down!" He then looked to the backseat where the twins were still sobbing and hollering.

"Y'all shut up!" he bellowed but they kept at it. This angered him further. "I said shut the fuck up, lil' mothafuckaz!" His frightful eyes looked from one twin to the other, but his husky voice poisoned their hearts with crippling fear. They were so horrified that they couldn't stop their sobbing and hollering.

"Oh, you lil' niggaz got heart, huh? You wanna test my G? Alright."

Tat! Tat!

The suddenly burst of gunfire startled homeboy behind the wheel of the Explorer. Looking over his shoulder and out of the driver side window, he saw his partner hauling ass from the station wagon. His eyes zeroed in on the backseat of the station wagon and he saw the O'Connor twins slumped dead in the backseat of the station wagon with big ass holes in their chest, eyes staring off to the side at nothing. The masked man with the Ak-47 hopped into the passenger seat and slammed the door closed.

"Awww, no!" His eyes went big and his mouth quivered seeing the gruesome sight. He looked over to his partner and grabbed his by the front of his shirt, shaking his heatedly. "What the fuck did you do, huh? What the fuck did you do?"

"Get cho mothafucking hands offa me, nigga," he scowled and smacked his hand down.

"Nigga, what the fuck you do that for?!" Homeboy behind the wheel asked.

"Never leave witnesses!" He retorted, switching hands with the Ak-47. "Now, drive this mothafucka!" He smacked the dashboard of the truck and it burned rubber from the crime scene.

Urrrrrrk!

The SUV blew past intersections with traffic cameras flashing on it. Its passengers didn't have shit to worry about though, because they still had on their masks and their ride was stolen.

***

Pulling upon a residential street, the masked men heard the ghetto bird approaching from above. Abandoning their weapons, they adopted their rental. Once they were out from under the shadow of the police helicopter, their heart beats slowed to a steady pace and they relaxed.

"Whoo!" Wameek shouted excitedly, punching the ceiling of the rental. He was high off of the work they had just put in. "We did that shit, nigga." He lit up a Newport, took a pull, and then blew smoke. Thereafter, he looked over to his little cousin and could tell something was bothering him. "Fuck wrong with chu, nigga?" He frowned, looking him up and down with flaring nostrils.

"Those were some lil' kids, man." Fear pulled a Newport from Wameek's pack, slipping it between his lips. "You didn't have to kill them lil' niggaz, fuck they gon' do? Tell? We masked up so we're good." He lit up the cancer stick with the rental car's cigarette lighter, then punched it back into its slot.

"Man, fuck them cracker's kids, Blood! They should have shut the fuck up when I told 'em to. If they had they'd still be alive." Wameek's eyebrows arched and his nose scrunched up. Fear didn't say a word. He just took a pull from his Joe and then blew the smoke into his face. Wameek disregarded his cousin's disrespect because now wasn't the time to check his ass. He was sure that he'd get his chance to holler at him later.

Fear turned the stereo up on Ghetto Child by Curtis Mayfield. He then lay back in his seat, coasting the rental through the city streets and taking pulls of his cigarette.

The neighborhood that he was cruising through reflected on the windshield of his vehicle. He had glassy eyes having seen the kids his relative had murdered laid up like that. His heart bled for their young lives that had been taken from the shady world all too soon. There wasn't any doubt in his mind that Wameek was going to be a problem, a problem that he may have to get rid of permanently.

The next day

It had been a couple of months since Fear had saw Master Kenneth Hahn, the man that had introduced him to the Kung Fu style of fighting as well as a few others. The young nigga had always been a fan of old kung fu movies like Lady Snow Blood, The White Lotus, The Street Fighter, etc, and wanted desperately to learn the arts. It took some convincing, but he finally managed to get Big Al to agree to let him take lessons. He and Master Hahn clicked like safety belts when they first met. The old man took a liking to him above all the other students. It was something about the young man that reminded him of himself. Monday through Friday from 3 o'clock until 7:30 p.m. you could catch AJ down at Hahn 's School of Discipline and Martial Arts.

Fear pulled up outside of his old teacher's house in Italia's BMW and murdered the engine. Taking the key out of the ignition, he threw open the door and hopped out. He came around the vehicle stuffing the keys into his pocket and jogging toward the house. He hopped the gate of the driveway and landed on his feet like a cat, before trekking the rest of the way. When he finally reached the end of the driveway, he came across the glass house where he could see someone moving around. Fear entered the glass house pulling the door shut behind him. Hahn had his back to him. He couldn't quite see what he was doing but he thought that maybe he could be trimming a tree or something. Smiling devilishly and licking his lips, the young nigga crept over to some nearby flowerpots where he spotted a bow and arrows. He grabbed the bow and picked up one of the arrows. Taking an expertise stance, he lifted the bow and pulled the arrow which had a jagged spear, back on the string. Shutting his left eye, he took aim at his mentor's back. His hand slightly shook as he held firm to the lethal weapon, waiting for the perfect time to let it go. For a time he listened to Hahn as he hummed the tune of the Japanese music that was playing. When Fear heard the voice in his head tell him now, he released the arrow.

Thoomp!

The arrow whistled through the air. Hahn went right along humming the tune seemingly oblivious to what was happening. Suddenly, his left ear slightly jumped and he stopped humming, eyes shooting to their corners. The arrow was about to pierce his back until he whipped around and snatched it out of the air. Holding the arrow in his clenched fist, he looked at it then snapped it in half with his thumb, letting both halves hit the floor. When his eyes looked up and met Fear's, he was smiling. A slight smile formed across his lips as well.

"I see you still got it old man," Fear applauded.

"Once you get it you'll never lose it." He turned around and he went back to trimming the Bonzie tree, humming. "What brings you here, Alvin Son?" He nipped at the tree wearing an amused expression on his face.

"Nothing, just thought I'd drop by and holla at chu," Fear told him, looking around at all of plants decorating the glass house. There were a variety of plants inhabiting the spacious place. Hidden within the plants were cannabis plants that were the richest green. Over against the fall corner was a homemade waterfall that added to the serene feeling that the place brought. Fear felt like he was in the tropics somewhere with the sun beating down on his back.

"Really? You drove way down to Paramount just to holla at me?" He cracked a smirk, looking at him amusingly.

"Yep, I was at this old Mexican boss type of nigga'z crib when I saw you in a picture there," he claimed, fondling the leaf of a plant, trying to see if what he'd said would garner his curiosity.

"Yeah? What was his name?" Hahn went about the task of cutting the Bonzie tree, humming the tune of a Japanese folk song as he did so.

"Gustavo." He looked up at him, seeing him stop trimming the tree. "I didn't know, you were a made man, how come you didn't tell me? I probably could have pulled rank and…"

"No!" Hahn spat sharply with a scowl, sitting the small set of clippers aside. "I wasn't a part of his organization; I was his clean up man. I took out the trash, done all of his dirty work."

"What happened then? What got chu to stop? Old age?" he guessed.

"Old age? I'm in my prime. I'm in the greatest shape of my life. I can still lay it down if it's called for." When he said this Fear studied his physique. He was a scrawny man but he was cut up, his muscles were well defined. He was built like a young Bruce Lee in the Enter the Dragon movie. "If I came to see you, then I was the last person you saw." His deathly serious eyes betrayed the evil that lurked behind them. Hidden behind them were the screaming faces of his countless victims as well as their stories. "I filled each and every contract. Most believe that I'm either dead or have up and vanished. My name is still spoken of in some of the roughest and toughest ghettos there are."

Fear nodded his understanding. "I started to drop your name figuring that you could put me where I need to be with this dude."

"You mentioned my name?" He pulled off his gloves and threw them on the table, approaching his protégé. "Why the fuck would you do that?" He grabbed him by the front of his shirt and slammed him up against the wall, causing him to bump his head. He winced and when he peeled his eyelids back open, Hahn 's face was twisted into hatred. "Why in the hell would you wanna do something like that, huh?" He angled his head, gritting his teeth as his pupils burst into flaming balls. He was heated like a mothafucka.

"I didn't do shit," Fear spat back, staring him in his eyes defiantly.

"Liarrr!" Hahn roared back. He felt his hot breath and his spittle hit his face.

"Master Hahn , I love you like a father, but I swear on my life and everything that I love, if you don't get your goddamn hands off of me, you and I are gon' have a situation." The men stayed locked into an intense gave for a time before teacher released student, breaking it. He apologized as he watched his protégé straightened out his clothes.

"I'm sorry, Alvin Son," He spoke humbly, stuffing his pipe with Kush and lighting it up. He sucked on the end of it and produced clouds of smoke.

"You and Gustavo gotta beef?" Fear frowned, folding his arms across his chest.

He blew the smoke out of his nose and mouth. Nodding, he said, "Yes. He has a one million dollar bounty out on my head."

Fear's eyes widened with surprise and he whistled at the thought of that much coming through his hands. He figured that his teacher must have done some pretty foul shit for a nigga to put that kind of paper on his head.

"Why does he have such a hard-on for you?"

"I was having an affair with his daughter," Hahn admitted, looking up at him as high as he could ever be. His eyes were hooded and red webbed. That shit inside of his pipe had him mellowed out. It was like his life was on cruise control.

"Big deal." He shrugged. "She was a grown ass woman, wasn't she?"

He shook his head no and said, "She was seventeen."

Fear hung his head and shook it. "Damn, Hahn , seventeen? No wonder why this nigga wants your head."

"Yeah, I know it was fucked up, but we really loved one another. I mean, I loved her but I loved my wife more."

"Wait a minute, loved her?" he looked up with confusion on his face. "You mean, she's..."

Hahn shut his eyes and nodded before he could finish. He then took a deep breath and went on to tell the story.

***

Three of Gustavo's men kicked in Hahn's door catching him and his wife off guard. Before he could mount a defense, they were on him beating him down and zapping him with cattle prods. Once they were done with him, they planted him in a chair and duct taped his wrists and ankles to it.

"Uuuhhh," a barely conscious Hahn moaned, eyes hooded and head bobbling about.

"Duct tape her ass to that chair over there!" The top dawg of the masked men ordered, pointing his Glock at Hahn 's wife. In the other hand, he held a cattle prod. The third masked man snatched the wife up and planted her ass in a chair, duct taping her to it as well.

"Ahhhhh! Somebody helllp uussss!" She threw her head back and screamed at the top of her lungs.

"Shut dat bitch up!" The head nigga commanded.

Bwap!

One of the men cracked her upside of the head with that steel and her head leant to the side. Her eyes rolled to their whites and she moaned in pain. One of the men held her head upright by her chin while the other smacked a strip of duct-tape over her mouth.

"Don't chu hurt her, don't chu dare hurt her!" Hahn roared, mad dogging the men with a snarl. He looked like he'd gone feral. "Arrrrrgh! Ahhh! Gahhh!" His eyes stretched open as wide as they'd go and so did his mouth. The poor bastard was shocked several times with cattle prods in his sides and torso. Tak! Tak! Tak! Tak! The prods sounded as volts surged through them, ready to be used if he decided to buck again.

"Put in the tape!" The top dawg demanded of one of his goons. As one was putting the tape inside of the VCR, he turned to Hahn . "Gustavo wants you to watch this, every second of every minute of this footage. He wants you to experience the heartbreak he had seeing his daughter do this. Then he's going to experience yours once we murder your wife in front of you." He sat the cattle prod down on the arm of the couch and pulled his cell phone out of his back pocket. He danced it before his eyes and tossed it over to the goon behind his wife. He caught it and began filming through the camera phone.

"No, please, she doesn't have anything to do with this! Just let her go! It's me that he wants."

"Quit your bitching and face the punishment for your violation like a man."

Crack!

He punched him in the jaw sending a spray of blood into the air. He then picked up the remote control and turned the volume up as loud as it would go. The TV was so loud that it resonated throughout the house. Afterwards, he tossed the remote aside. Smiling wickedly, he looked from Hahn to the screen of the flat-screen. "Don't miss a single beat, pay close attention, asshole!" Hahn looked ahead and watched the flat-screen attentively, occasionally spitting blood on the floor.

A beautiful girl with dark flat-ironed hair and skin the color of a walnut appeared on the screen. Her eyes were so puffy and bloodshot it led one to believe she'd been punched in them repeatedly. She sniffled and wiped her dripping nose with a curled finger. Biting down on her bottom lip, she took a deep breath and pressed to move on.

"You lied to me, Kenneth; you promised me that we'd be together forever just as long as I got rid of the baby. And even though I didn't want to I did 'cause I didn't want chu to leave me. I loved you; I loved you down to the core of my very soul, so I did the inexcusable. I killed my baby, I aborted my unborn child." She bowed her head as she broke down sobbing, teardrops trickling to the floor. She looked back up into the camcorder, taking another deep breath. "You deceitful bastard, you promised that you'd leave her for me, you toyed with my heart…"

While she was talking and everyone seemed to be solely focused on her, Hahn slowly began working his wrist loose from its restraint. When he looked to his right, he found his wife's scared eyes watching him. He gave her a nod which signaled to her that he had everything under control. She returned the gesture. Hahn zeroed in on the top dawg who was standing beside him, clutching his Glock.

"Do you have any idea what you've done? Do you? I hear the baby at night crying, please, don't kill me, mommy. Please, I'm sorry for whatever I did!" She hung her head whimpering and hollering. Sniffling and wiping her eyes, she looked back up into the camera lens. "My baby's alone now. She needs me so I'm going to join her. If you have any sympathy or compassion for what you drove me to do, I'll see you there with us shortly."

"You watching this?" The leader looked to Hahn right when he'd freed his hand from the duct-tape of the arm of the chair. He'd thought he'd been caught, but he hadn't.

"Please, please, I can't bear to see her like this! Cut it off, I beg of you." He looked up at him with pleading eyes that desperately wanted mercy.

"Notta chance and if you shut your eyes, you'll neva open them again." He scowled and squared his jaws causing them to pulsate.

Smack!

The nigga standing on the opposite side of Hahn smacked the shit out the back of his head. His head snapped in his direction. He was wearing lines across his forehead, looking stun. "You made this mess, mothafucka. Now grow a pair and watch it before you die!" He then focused his attention back on the TV. Hahn took in what every one of Gustavo's men was doing. They all were locked on the television while his wife had her eyes closed looking like she was praying as tears cascaded down her face. He looked to the screen to find Caroline standing on a chair and looping a noose around her neck. Throwing her head back, she shut her eyes and counted to three silently. Right when she'd jumped, Hahn snatched his wrist free from the tape and snatched the banger from out of the leader's hand. Turning it on him, he squeezed off twice into his chest. He then whipped around to the nigga standing beside him, shooting him in his torso and dropping him to the floor. When he looked ahead, the goon guarding his wife had just lowered the cellular he was using to film everything to his side and had pressed his ratchet to the back of her skull.

"Noooooo!" he bellowed pointing his weapon and pulling the trigger.

Blowl! Blowl! Blowl! Pop! Pop! Pop!

Hahn grimaced taking one in his shoulder and toppling over in his chair. He hit the floor with a thud and looked around from where he lay, his one free hand moving about with the head bussa. He spotted the nigga he'd gave two to the chest, staggering forward and holding his bleeding wounds. The man eventually crashed to the floor, lying on the side of his face breathing hard, blowing debris up from the floor.

"Hold on, honey, I'm coming." Hahn sat his tool beside him on the floor and tore the duct tape that kept his other hand bounded. When he leaned up to tear the tape from around his ankles, he saw his wife still in her chair lying on her side with half of her head missing. Horror was etched on her face, eyes as big as silver dollars and mouth stretched wide open. She was dead.

"Oh, why? Why?" He whined and whimpered looking up at the ceiling questioning a higher power, tears constantly flooding down his cheeks. "I'm so sorry, honey. I'm so sorry." Hahn finally tore the tape from his ankles and came up off of the floor, picking up his burner. He walked over to his wife, angling his head as he stared down at her. He snorted back snot and the tears fell faster. Smacking a hand over the lower half of his face, his shoulders rocked as he muffled his sobbing. The moans and groans coming from his rear contracted his face with animosity. He gripped the metal in his hand tightly and turned around; advancing in the direction of the mothafuckaz that still had the audacity to still be breathing. Their eyes widen with fear as his shadow eclipsed them and he banished them to hell.

Blowl! Blowl! Blowl! Blowl!

After wiping his finger prints off of the murder weapon, Hahn tossed it aside and attended to his wife. Down on his knees, he combed his hand through her bloody hair and kissed her on the side of the face before shutting her eyes.

Next, he packed a quick bag, grabbed some money and called 9-1-1 on his way out of the door.

Present

"It's all my fault that she's gon'," Hahn admitted with tears building in his glassy eyes. His body rocked with emotion as if he was standing butt naked in a blizzard. Sniffling, he held up his trembling hands and continued, "I swear to you, Alvin Son, I would move Heaven and Earth with my bare hands to be able to feel the warmth of her embrace and the alluring scent of her perfume, just one last time." He held up a quaking finger. "But now it's too late. That chance is as dead as she is," he stated regretfully and hung his head. His body jerked violently as he sobbed with a hand over his nose and mouth, teardrops falling from his grieving eyes rapidly. Taking a deep breath, he wiped the wetness from his eyes with a curled finger. Seeing his mentor in such great pain had Fear feeling for him. He felt hotness sting his eyes, but he wouldn't allow his emotions to take him. Nah, this was his teacher's time to grieve. He needed this release all to himself and he was going to let him have it. Fear pulled a red bandana from his back pocket and passed it to him. Hahn wiped his face and nose with it and folded it in half to go back over his cheeks a second time.

"You'll be alright…" Fear went to grasp his shoulder, but his head shot up. Looking at his hand like it was a disease, he scowled and gritted.

"Don't ," he told him, not wanting to feel like he was being pitied.

"Alright." Fear threw up his hands in surrender and slowly backed away.

"I trust that you will keep my whereabouts to yourself, or are you looking to collect that cheek." He went to draw two gleaming silver, ninja stars from his sleeves.

"I would never betray you, Master Hahn, like I've already said, you're like a father to me," he spoke from the heart, kind of hurt that the old man would even begin to think that he'd sell him out. Hanging his head and stuffing his hands into his pockets, he made his stride toward the door.

"Alvin Son," Hahn called after his protégé and he turned around. "I'm sorry. It's just that having been in the business that I was in; you grow accustomed to not trusting a soul."

"You can trust me," he swore. "I have a code and principles that I'll never betray. It's loyalty over everything with me."

Hahn nodded and asked, "See you soon?"

"Yeah," he nodded back and went about his business.

CHAPTER SIX
2010

It was night in Sin City and all that could be heard was the pleasured moans of a woman and the grunting of a man as wet flesh slapped against one another. Her satisfied face showed through the glass of the ceiling to floor window of the $1200 dollar a night presidential suite. Her head was tilted back as her hair was pulled in a tight hold by a chocolate hand. Her tits jumped forth with each thrust that her lover provided upon his exit and re entree of her warm, moist womb. While one hand held her hair in a firm hold, he licked his fingertips with his hot, wet tongue. He rubbed that small flap of meat that was nestled between her southern lips as he worked her from behind vigorously. This heightened the sex for her, driving her to scream and shout as that hot liquid avalanched down her legs, dripping onto the rich cream carpet.

"Haa! Haa! Haa! Haa!" He breathed heavily, his hot breath blowing against her sweaty back. His face was twisted into a scowl as he locked eyes with her through the window, transfixed on her face as he gave her something long and hard. Each slam of his thick engorged member hit an air pocket in her pussy causing it to fart and spray her juices. "Ahh! Ahh! Ahh!" He grunted, squaring his jaws and lapping at her ample ass, faster and faster. His mound met with her buttocks and made a noise that sounded like thunderous hand claps.

He gripped her hair tighter and yanked her head back, making her holler louder than ever. "Ahhhhhhh!"

Smack! Smack! Smack! He hit that shit from the back, body growing hotter, sweat dripping from his brows. "Ahhh, yeah, yeah, the pussy's good! The pussy's real good!"

"Ah, yes, yes, baby! Fuck me, fuck the shit outta me! Ooooooh!" Her eyes turned over to their whites, causing her to look possessed. Her mouth hung open as the sound was fucked out of her ass. Homie was giving her that work, long stroking that thang.

"You like that shit?" He rasped, smacking her ass.

"Yeah!" Her voice went up an octave.

"Huh? Huh?" He asked louder. "I can't hear yo' mothafucking ass!" Smack! He smacked her left butt cheek and she cried out for more, licking her top lip.

"Oh, yes, yes, God! I love it! I fucking love it!"

He gripped her by the hips, angling his head and looking down. He bit down on his bottom lip watching his dick, plow into her rapidly. Hot droplets of sweat rained from his brows and splashed on her already drenched back. The lovers perspiration had them shining like they were covered in crushed diamonds.

"I'm 'bout to cum!" She whined and smiled, hands pressed up against the fogging glass as she threw that luscious ass back into him hurriedly. His meat massaged her slick insides, spear heading her toward her most explosive orgasm.

He held his wrists at his back and enjoyed the view of her buttocks colliding with his pelvis. Each time she threw that thang against him, he slightly folded at the waist. It got so good to him that he felt his shaft swell and he threw his head back. His eyes turned into slits and he mouth formed an O. He hissed like a snake and clenched his jaws, looking down at that fat chunky booty swallowing his meat and spitting it back out.

"Ahhhh, fuck! Hold up, baby, let me hit that shit!" He clutched her thighs firmly, looking down and fucking her middle intensely, their forms making thunderous claps each time that they met. Her hollering grew louder and louder, as both of their faces balled up. Suddenly, he snatched his glistening erection from her V and jerked his dick. Back and forth his hand went traveled his girth until he finally released warm mayonnaise on his conquest's ass and back. "Shhhhiiiit," his lips peeled apart, showcasing the webs of saliva inside of his mouth. His face morphed into a scowl. He thought he'd never stop busting for as many of his children as he was shooting out of the head of his penis. Having finishing emptying his nut sack, he rubbed his limp member back and forth across delicious heart shaped ass, twitching having let loose of the greatest orgasm in his life. He collapsed to the floor as naked as the day he was born. His entire body shined from perspiration as his chest rose and fell rapidly.

"Haa! Haa! Haa! Haa!" He wore a smile on his lips as he lifted his head up from the carpet to see the love of his life. He found her looking over her shoulder at the jizz he'd plastered her butt with. She smiled and looked up at her boo, blowing him a kiss from her palm before taking off toward the bathroom. He cheeks danced one at a time with each step she took with her bare feet. When she made it to the doorway of the bathroom, she stopped and turned around to him. She gave him a seductive look while twisting a nail at the corner of her teeth. Taking her hand from her mouth, she used her finger to signal him over, curling and uncurling it. She disappeared into the bathroom and made a right toward the shower. He jumped up on his feet and darted into the bathroom, slamming door shut behind him.

Fear and Italia sexed in the shower before drying one another off and getting dressed in their undergarments. Italia, wearing her bra, panties and kimono, sat on the edge of the bed applying lotion to her arms and legs. Fear leaned up against the doorway of the kitchen with his arms folded across his chest. A smirk was on his lips as he looked on admiringly, his lady was hands down the finest he had ever laid eyes on.

"Let me help you out, babe." He made his way over to her, his black silk pajama's hanging around his hips and showing off that muscular V that lead to his shaved mound. She marveled him from where she sat and licked her teeth, like she was trying to figure out what she tasted like. Even with all of those hideous scars over his body he was still one sexy ass man to her. Truthfully, his marred form didn't bother her in the least bit. In fact, they added to his sex appeal and heightened her attraction to him.

Fear kneeled down to her and looked up into her eyes, outstretching her leg. He took the bottle of lotion from her and dabbed some into his palm. He rubbed his palms together. Taking his time, he rubbed down each of her legs and massaged them gently. She threw her head back and shut her eyes, moaning delightfully as she enjoyed the feel of his strong hands. His palms traveled up and down her legs, over her feet, to the bottoms of them. Once he was done, he made sure to rub down her thighs, getting closer and closer to her warm vagina, feeling the heat expelling from it. Her clit stiffened and her pussy moistened, feeling how close he was getting to her womanhood. She peeled her eyelids back open and looked down at him, grinning at him with those enticing lips of hers.

"You betta stop before you get something started now." She gave him the warning, but hoped that he continued his efforts of seduction.

"Oh, that's exactly what I'm trying to do." He stood erect and laid her back on the bed, peeling her kimono from off of her shoulders. She closed her eyes as he placed kisses as soft as rose pedals on her collarbone and shoulder, causing her to shudder like a cold breeze. He licked her up her throat to her chin and gave her a little tongue as he kissed her mouth. While their mouths were massaging one another in a slow building rhythm, he slipped his hands inside of her panties and began to rub on that small flap of meat between her pussy lips. She gasped feeling her coochie become wet. Her body met with tremors and she begged him for something that would put out that fire of passion burning in her.

"Ssssss, babe, put it in…Oooooh, put it in, please," she pleaded with shut eyes and he bit down gently on her bottom lip, pulling it softly. He then licked her mouth and pierced her lips with his tongue, kissing her hard as his fingers groped her creamy center. "Ah! Ah! Ah! Ah!" She got out in between kisses, looking down at his hand like she was seeing something scary. That wasn't true though. Nah, she was about to orgasm.

"Ooooooooooh, Faaaaatherrrr!" She mashed her eyelids together and threw her head back, mouth trembling. Her entire form quaked feeling that addictive sensation that every woman loved so much. "Jesus, Mary and Joseph, whooooo!" She looked back up and met his lips for another kiss. "I love you."

"I love you, too." He took her delicate hand and kissed it, staring up into her eyes.

She smiled.

Knock! Knock! Knock! Knock!

"Room service," the voice came from the opposite side of the door.

"You betta get that," she cooed.

"I am, gimmie some lip first though," he spoke with lowered eyes and an alluring voice. She closed their distance and they kissed. He pecked her one last time on the lips before getting to his feet. While he went to answer the door, she dipped off to the bathroom to freshen herself up.

Fear opened the door and allowed the connoisseur in with the pushcart. He pushed the cart inside of the dining room and when he turned around, Fear was tossing him a black chip.

"Always bet on black, my man." He patted him on his shoulder as he headed for the door.

"Thank you, sir." The connoisseur nodded.

"Don't mention it." Fear shut the door and locked it behind him.

"Smells good," Italia claimed, walking out of the bathroom tying her kimono around her waist.

"Sure does," Fear replied, opening a bottle of red wine and pouring up their respective glasses. Once he was done, he hurried around the table and pulled out her chair for her. When she sat down and scooted her seat up to the table, he took the sterling silver covers off of the entrees one by one. The first meal was his which consisted of a lobster, baked potato, medium rare steak and a salad. The second meal was hers. It was lasagna, garlic bread sticks and a salad. On the side, there was a bowl of sausage and potato soup which she loved. Italia and her man closed their eyes and inhaled the tantalizing smells of the food before them. Fear sat the covers off to the side and sat down at the table, gathering the silverware he'd need to indulge in his meal. His lady was following right behind him.

"Mmmmm. This is good, this is real good." Fear pointed his fork at the steak he'd taken a bite out of with a mouthful of food. He picked up his glass of wine and took a couple of sips.

"This is too, you wanna try mine?" Italia asked, one side of her jaw swollen with food as she chewed, twisted spaghetti around her fork.

He took another sip of wine to wash the food down and nodded. Next, he leaned over the table opening his mouth to receive the food. Once he got it into his mouth, he sat back down, chewing his food and savoring it. The expression on his way told her that he thought that lasagna was as good as she claimed.

"That shit is good." He pointed at the lasagna on her plate.

"Told you." She smiled, still eating.

Fear went to take another bite of his steak when his cellular rang. Looking to the device's screen as it lay on the table, he saw his mother's name and tried to decide whether or not he was going answer are not. See, he hadn't been spoken with his mother or his father since that night he'd left them. They tried getting into contact with him several times, but he didn't have any holler for him.

"Hey, momma," Fear spoke into the cell phone dryly, his eyes were shifty as he listened to what he was being told. "What?" Bang! "Ouch!" He shot to his feet and hit his knee of the table, he wiped his mouth with the cloth napkin. His brows wrinkled as he turned around, walking away and toss it on the table. A frowning Italia watched him from where she was perched. After taking a sip of wine, she sat the glass down on the table and walked over to her man. Her hand slid up and down his back in an attempt to comfort him.

"Is everything alright?" she asked and he threw up a finger for her to give him a minute. From the expression on his face, she could tell that he was seriously focused on the conversation at hand.

"Ma, I'll be there tonight, okay? I'm on my way now. I love you, too." He disconnected the call and turned to his lady, running a hand down his face. He took a deep breath and blew hot air, while she continued to rub his back. A look of concern was plastered on her face as she stared into his eyes waiting to see what was going on back home.

"Talk to me, Alvin."

"I gotta get back home," he walked away from her and grabbed his shirt, slipping it back over his head.

"What's the matter, baby?"

"I'll explain everything on the flight back," he assured her zipping up his Levi's 501 jeans. "Don't bother packing shit. I'm in a rush, just slip on yo' clothes so that we can get ghost."

"Alright, sweetheart." She moved to start getting dressed.

As soon as Italia slipped on her clothes, they were out of the hotel in a flash. They alerted the chauffer of them flying back and threw him a healthy tip. Two hours later, their jet had landed and a stair ladder had been pushed up to the opened hatch of the aircraft. Fear came hurrying down the steps holding his lady's hand while his other held his cell phone to his ear.

"Ma, the flight just landed, we're on our way now, okay?" He spat into the cellular like automatic gunfire, he had to make it home before it was too late. If he thought what would happen occurred before he'd gotten there he'd spend the rest of his life hating himself. "Alright." He disconnected the call and when he looked up, a black stretch Lincoln Town Car was pulling up. The chauffer was well aware of the emergency, so he hopped out and ran around to the opposite side of the vehicle to open the back door. Fear allowed his lady to slide inside before going in behind her and slamming the door shut. The driver hopped back in behind the wheel and drove off to their destination.

A half an hour later

Screeeeech!

Fear was throwing open the back door before the chauffer could make it around to him. Holding his boo's hand; he jumped out of the limo and ran towards his parents' house. The front door swung open as he cleared half of the yard. He found the silhouette of his mother standing in the doorway holding herself. Her body slightly quivered from sobbing.

"Momma."The rebellious young man embraced his mother, hugging her against his body. Hearing her wailing against his shirt and feeling her tears soil his fabric brought tears to his eyes. He could only imagine feeling what she was at this point and time. Truthfully, he was terrified of facing what he hadn't a choice but to deal with. The mere thought of it made him weak in his knees but he had to save face for his mother and the love of his life.

Still holding on to her son, Verna took three deep breaths before pulling away from him. She wiped her tears away with a curled finger and sniffled. When she looked to Italia and saw her crying too, it touched her. The girl was as good as family in her eyes.

"Come here, sweetie." She opened her arms and mustered up a halfhearted smile. Wiping away the wetness from her eyes, Italia swiped her nose and hugged her future mother in law. They both shared a mutual grievance and sobbed before they broke their embrace.

"How are you doing, ma?" Italia asked concerned.

Verna took a deep breath before replying. "The best I can under these circumstances." She exasperated and blinked back the water in her eyes, trying to be strong. "Whewww, Lord, gimmie strength." Her head tilted up to the ceiling to The Man upstairs as she held her hands together in prayer. Afterwards, she took a couple of deep breaths again to calm herself, wiping the dampness from the corner of her eyes.

"Ma, I wanna…" Fear nodded down the hall where his parents' bedroom was. He didn't have to say what he was getting at because he and his mother already knew what he had in mind. It was what any child would want to do in his shoes…make things right.

"Go right ahead, son, he's waiting for you." She smiled and patted him on the back. He closed his eyes and took a deep breath, licking his licks. Once he'd gathered his wits, he started for his parents' bedroom. It was time to put the beef to bed that had kept him up so many nights.

Fear turned the knob and pushed the door of his father's bedroom open gently. Almost as if he was attempting to sneak in and steal something. Sticking his head inside, he found his old man lying down with his hands resting on his waist. He was a far cry from the six foot three, 260 pound man that he called the giant when he was little boy. He was merely a skeleton with skin lying over it. It was a terribly sad sight to see him like that. In fact, it brought tears to his eyes that threatened to spill over their rims. He felt weak at the knees. He buckled a little and nearly fell, but quickly righted himself. A million and one thoughts trampled through his mind. This couldn't be real, this couldn't possibly be happening, but yes it was true…Superman was dying. *Not chu, pop, not chu*, he shook his head as his chin wrinkled and his bottom lip trembled. A small whimper escaped his lips as he watched his father clinging on for dear life, his chest slowly rising and falling. He was weak, really weak. It didn't even look like it was him lying down in that bed…it looked more like a corpse that someone had dressed up at a funeral parlor.

The noise that he made prompted his father to look over to him.

"Verna?" Big Al called out hoarsely for his wife, looking about. "Baby, is that you?"

Hastily, Fear wiped the tears from his face using his hands and shirt. He sniffled and wiped his dripping nose before brushing his hands off on his jeans. He licked his lips and cleared his throat before letting his presence be known.

"Nah, pop, it's not ma. It's me, your baby boy; AJ." Fear stepped into the bedroom, closing the door behind him.

"Hey, son," he mustered up a halfhearted smile. "How have you been?"

"I'm gucci, pop," Fear answered, pulling up a chair and sitting down at the side of the bed.

He lightly chuckled and said, "Junior, now you know I don't comprehend any of that slang y'all using today."

"My fault, it just means that I'm straight, is all."

"I see." He ogled the icy gold Jesus piece and the presidential Rolex adorning his son's wrist. "You're gonna have The Man all over you son…buying all of those nigga trinkets."

"Nigga trinkets, pop?" Creases appeared on his forehead.

Seeing the beads of sweat on his forehead, Fear dunk a folded washcloth into the bowl of water on the dresser and wrung it out, he then gently patted the perspiration from his forehead.

"Uh huh," he said, closing his eyes enjoying the soothing water against his forehead. "Shit that doesn't matter. Things that the black man buys that keep him poorer and the white man richer: big screen TVs, fancy cars, rims, clothes, jewelry. None of that mess will have any value in the long run, son. If you want my advice…invest in property. Own some land, that's the way to go."

Fear nodded and responded, "Will do."

"Tell me…what is it that you do for those dead presidents bulging outta your pocket there?" He spoke with his eyes closed. His revelation made his son look to the pocket of his jeans where a thick roll of Benjamin Franklins were stashed. He knew that they were there, but he didn't know that his father had taken noticed. That kind of fucked him up. His old man had always had a way of knowing things that he thought he was doing a good job hiding.

"Pop, you don't wanna know," he told him as he continued to pat his forehead with the folded washcloth.

"I know its illegal, that's for sure." His father went on. "And knowing those knuckleheaded nephews of mine that means drugs, which includes murder 'cause both of those go hand in hand in that game."

"Pop, I…"

"Shhhhhh, save your breath, son, you could never lie to me; maybe to your mother but never to me," he spoke honestly. "When Judgment Day comes and it's time to meet your Lord and Savior, you look 'em right in his eyes and you accept whatever fate he hands down." His eyes peeled open and he looked to his only son. "You stand there and be the man that I raised you to be. You hear me, Junior?"

"Yeah, pop." He nodded his head, eyes growing glassy.

Big Al went into a coughing fit, lifting his head slightly off of the bed and harping with his fist to his mouth. Seeing this, Fear picked up the pitcher of water and poured him a glass. He set the pitcher down on the dresser and brought the glass toward his father.

"Here you go, take a drink." His father laid his head back down on the pillow and he tilted the glass to his lips, watching as he drunk from it. He sat the glass down and he looked to the faded tattoo on the inside of his arm that was of the Superman symbol. His life was fading away just like the tattoo was…and it wouldn't be much longer before both of them were gone. Fear looked back up at his senior. He'd started harping and coughing again. Suddenly the realization of him really being gone struck him hard like an iron fist.

His father had always been a good man so he couldn't see how his God was going to take him out the way he was...cancer. Damn, that shit was eating his old man alive and it was killing him. Fear wished that cancer was a living, breathing man so he could go looking for him and cut his bitch ass down with that choppa for doing his pop in like he was. He understood that cancer was far from human so he'd take this issue up with the Lord Almighty instead. He'd hate HIM until the day he was lying in a coffin with his eyes closed and his hands overlapping one another.

Fear focused on Big Al as he laid his head back down against the pillow. He watched him as tears pooled in his eyes and threatened to fall. He quickly wiped them away not wanting his pop to see him vulnerable. Coming up he'd always taught him to keep a Poker Face so that no one would know what he was thinking or feeling.

He pulled his chair up closer to the bed and leaned forth taking his father's hand into his. He started off, "Pop, I know I haven't exactly been the best..."

"I know son, it's okay," Big Al cut him off. "It's alright. It's not like I was exactly the best father either."

"Nah, nah," he shook his head and gripped his hand tighter. "You were the best father that there ever was, or ever will be. You taught me so much, pop; stuff that I still use today. I'm so proud that you're my Dad and I'm so lucky to be your son. I wouldn't trade you in for nothing pop, nothing in the world..." He stopped himself. Closing his eyes, he tried to gather himself so that his voice wouldn't crackle and bare his raw emotions. Once he felt that he'd gotten his emotions in order, he continued. "I just wish...I just wish that I would have taken the time out to tell you how special you are to me and how much you mean to me, instead of waiting 'til now. I love you, pop...and I don't want chu to die, man...I need you..." he laid his head on his hand and sobbed silently so that he wouldn't hear him. Hot tears oozed out of his eyes and warmed his cheeks, eventually growing cold. He licked his lips and tasted the saltiness of them. His chest trembled as he sobbed as quietly as he could as to not draw his father's attention. The streets had christened him Fearless but that wasn't true. At least not at this moment it wasn't because as of right now he was scared...scared of losing the only man that he'd ever loved...his father.

"I need you, pop. Please, don't go." He looked back up at his old man, wiping his face with the back of one hand. "If you stay alive I swear to God, I'll give all of this up on the spot. I'll leave the game alone, I swear it," he spoke the truth with pink eyes and a drenched face. "I..." He cut himself short and his brows furrowed once he saw his old man staring up at the ceiling at something. His eyes were on the brink of spilling tears and his mouth was agape. Wondering what had captured his attention, he looked up in the direction that his father was but he didn't see anything. But he felt something and he knew that it was there...death.

"Junior," Big Al croaked.

"Yeah, pop?"

"If you love me as much as you say you do, I need you to get up and walk away now."

"What's wrong, pop?"

"Son, please..." he swallowed his spit, daring not to blink his eyes or his tears would fall. He couldn't allow his son to see him crying before he made his departure from this world to the next. For as long as he could remember, his baby boy had always looked up to him as if he was a superhero. And he wanted to leave that image that he'd depicted of him inside of his head unscathed. In his final hour , this is what mattered to him the most.

"Okay. Alright, pop." Fear's voice crackled and his eyes turned moist. He could feel the crack making its way down his heart, splitting it down the middle. Holding his senior's hand with both of his, he kissed it lovingly. He then stood up and swept his hand over his forehead, kissing him above his brows. As soon as he turned his back, Big Al closed his eyes and tears shot down his chocolate cheeks. His throat moved up and down his neck as he swallowed and expelled his last breath. Hearing it as he headed out of the bedroom, Fear shuddered and sobbed. He didn't dare turn around because he didn't want to see his pop like that. Coming out of the bedroom, he closed the door as he crossed the threshold. The young hustler found his mother standing in the hallway eyes pink and face wet. She looked into her only son's eyes for confirmation of her husband's death. He shook his head slightly and her hands cupped her face as she began crying aloud. He rushed over to her and wrapped his arms around her. They both cried long, loud and hard.

Looking over his mother's shoulder, he locked eyes with Italia and waved her over. She joined them in one big hug.

There's nothing in this world like family.

CHAPTER SEVEN
2010

Fear was alright during the days leading up to his old man's funeral. He made the arrangements; picked the coffin, the suit he was to be buried in, the flowers, etc. He seemed to be like his old self, but on August 7th all of that changed because he knew that it would be the last day he'd see his father above ground. He made it through both viewings of the body, but when it came to the burial at the cemetery, he had a hard time controlling his emotions and unfortunately it got the best of him. Everyone had left besides himself, his mother, Italia and Big Sexy.

When the last of the dirt was thrown over the plot, Fear lost control of himself.

"Nooooooo!" He screamed aloud, eyes wide and spit flying from his lips. He ran and dove onto the pile, clawing up the land like a dog trying to find a bone he'd buried. "You're not dead; you're not dead, pop! You can't be!" His arms moved at a fast and steady pace, throwing dirt behind him. The tears flowed rapidly down his cheeks, his eyes red webbed and glassy.

"Please, pop, please, be alive, man! I need you!" He sobbed, tears rolling down his face and splashing on the dirt.

"Oh my God, AJ!" Verna threw her hands over her face and wailed, body rocking hard with grief. Seeing her son in this state really fucked with her. The death of her husband and his father had shaken their world and turned it upside down. Her baby boy's unadulterated behavior was a testament to this. She'd never seen him in this state before and she knew that if they were ever able to bring him back, that he would never be the same again.

"Baby!" Italia hollered, tears running and mixing with the rain. She chased after her grieving man. The young nigga was far gone and he needed her now more than ever. "Alvin." She got down on the dirt that had now formed into mud, smudging her heels and dress doodoo brown. She grabbed a hold of one of his arms with both of her hands. But he used his free one to keep clawing on the pile hurriedly, sending dirt flying every which way. Once he saw that he wasn't getting the job done any faster with her holding onto his other arm, he turned around to her trying to push her off of his arm.

"Babe, stop! He's gone!" She hollered. "I'm sorry, I'm so sorry."

"Get the fuck off of me! You don't know what you're talking about. He's still alive! He's gonna suffocate in there! Ugh!" He shoved her off of him and she fell back onto the mud. Mud covered her hands all of the way up her arms. All she could do was watch as her best friend and lover tried to dig up his father's coffin. Her chest quaked and her head bobbed, as tears cascaded down her face. Her man was hurting. His father's death did more damage to him than an AK-47 bullet could. The sad part about it was, the way he was performing she didn't know if there was anything that she could do to ease his pain and turmoil. For now she'd do the best she could and leave the rest in God's hands. Truthfully, that was all that she could do.

"AJ, stop! Stop it, son!" Verna called out to her son, but he couldn't hear her. His mind was solely focused on digging up his old man and proving to them all he was still alive and well.

She started to go after him but Big Sexy stepped up, placing an assuring hand on her shoulder that he would take care of her first born. He'd just got done seeing away the last of the mourners when he heard his closest friend's cry.

"Haa! Haa! Haa! Haa!" Fear breathed heavily, hard at work digging up the ground. Half of his suit was covered in mud, but he didn't give two shits. He was concentrating on the task at hand. "Haa! Haa! Haa! I know you're alive, pop! And I'm gonna prove it! I'm gonna prove it to them all! Watch they'll see! They'll all see!" He had madness in his eyes that a person wearing a straight jacket and dwelling in a padded room would have. He danced on the tight rope of insanity and was losing his footing. If he didn't somehow pull himself together , there wasn't any doubt that he'd be lost to everyone that loved him.

"Stop this shit, man!" Big Sexy grasped his shoulder and he swung on him in a blind rage. Bwrap! The impact of the blow threw the giant's head back. When he brought his chin back down, he had bloody teeth. When Fear tried to strike him again, he caught his fist in his massive palm, closing his fingers around it tightly. Pact! He caught his second fist and squeezed it tight, hearing the bones in his hand crackling. Fear saw a red haze before his eyes and he gritted, dying to dismantle his right hand man. It was like he wasn't there any more, as if some evil spirit had taken possession of his body.

"Aye, look at me, fam, where are you?" Big Sexy bored into his eyes with intensity. He was searching his friend's soul trying to find where he was dwelling within himself because he for damn sure didn't know who this was standing before him.

"Fuck…you…grrrr!" He grimaced, feeling the pressure on both of his hands, they felt as if they were about to snap at any minute now.

"Get a hold of yourself, man. Yo' pops gone and ya motha needs you now more than ever," he told him in a hush tone. "Look at her, G, she'd hurting, bruh?" He threw his head toward his mother. When the young nigga looked, he found his lady and his mother hugged up, staring at him with tear streaked faces. Right then the angered expression slid off of his face and he blinked as if he was realizing where he was for the very first time. He whipped his head back around to his main man.

"I miss, pop, man." His voice cracked and his face twisted, bottom lip quivering and nose dripping. "I miss him so much already, Sexy. I want 'em back, I want my daddy back, fam." He sniffled and his body shook. "I'm fucked up without 'em, I don't know what I'm gon' do."

"Damn." Big Sexy shook his enormous head, his eyes turning glassy, seeing his right hand in so much pain. He wrapped his huge arms around him and the smaller man buried his face into the chest of his shirt, sobbing. His voice vibrated against his form, the noise coming in and out of sync. "It's okay, its gon' be alright eventually. I know you going through it, but chu gon' have to pull yourself together for yo' motha's sake. She needs you to be rock solid during a time like this." Looking to Italia and Verna, he motioned them over with an open palm. They didn't waste any time running over and forming a group hug where everyone shed their tears and mourned, except Big Sexy.

Days later

Although it was daylight outside, the living room was dark and the fireplace was burning. The golden orange flames licked up the wooden logs causing them to crackle and pop. The illumination of the fire casted Fear's shadow on the far wall and caused it to dance. The hustler sat on the couch punishing his liver with a fifth of Hennessy and staring down at a portrait of himself and his old man. In the photo he was seven years old and dressed in his little league uniform. A big Kool Aid smile was plastered on his youthful face as he held up a trophy bigger than himself.

Towering over him was Big Al with his hand over his shoulder. He wore a smile on his lips. Fear remembered that day like it was yesterday. It was one of his happiest. In fact, it was one of his father's proudest besides the day he'd gotten the acceptance letter from UCLA. He recalled his father bragging to all of his buddies one night while they were playing cards about how his baby boy was going to be someone that was going to make an impact on the world that everyone would never forget.

"Damn, pop, if I could I would switch places witchu in a heartbeat." He sat the portrait down beside him and turned the bottle up, his throat rolling up and down his neck as he guzzled the dark liquor, the bath of flames engulfing his stomach burning it up. Its spiciness caused his face to ball. He brought the bottle down from his lips and wiped the alcohol that dripped with his fist. As much as he detested liquor, he needed it to numb his emotions. The way he saw it drinking was his only way to cope with his reality.

Knock! Knock! Knock!

Rapping at the door resonated throughout the living room, but he ignored it. His eyes were trained on the flames of the fire as he was watching them dance, their silhouettes playing on the wall. Italia came down the staircase clutching a .45. Her hair was pulled back in a ponytail. She was dressed in a wife beater, skinny jeans and Timbs. Reaching the landing, she stole a glance at Fear. Seeing the hurt in his eyes as he watched the fire, she made a detour from the door and rubbed his head, pecking him on the top of it. Afterwards, she rubbed his shoulder and stepped to the front door, stealing a peek through the peephole to see who it was. Confirming the guest, she unchained and unlocked the door, pulling it open.

"Hey, sis." Big Sexy crossed the threshold into the house, kissing her on the side of the head affectionately.

His forehead crinkled as he looked around the living room, surprised to see all of the lights out being that it was broad daylight outside.

"Hey, Sex." She closed the door behind him. She turned around just in time to See Big Sexy about to sit down on the couch. "I'm gonna go make myself a drink. Do you want anything?"

"A Bud will do, sweetheart, if you got one."

"Yep, coming right up."

"Thanks."

"Don't mention it." She disappeared inside of the kitchen.

Once she was gone, he turned around to his friend and tapped him on his knee. He watched him take another swallow of alcohol and sit the bottle of Hennessy down on the coffee table. For the first time, he noticed his beaded hair and 5 o'clock shadow.

"'Sup?" Fear stared ahead, not bothering to make eye contact.

"I made sure yo' moms got on that plane to Connecticut to yo' Aunt's, like you asked."

"G' looking, family, a nigga really appreciate that."

"Notta problem," he replied. "I drop by the club and made sure everything was alright there too. I gotta admit, homie, that was a damn good investment."

"Yep."

Hearing someone enter the living room, Big Sexy looked up to see Italia carrying a Budweiser beer for him, the bottle sweating from its coldness. She passed it to him and he thanked her before she journeyed back up the staircase.

"Look, man, I know you fucked up with all that has happened to yo' father and all but yo' people need you out there. You gotta get back on it, fam, don't let niggaz see you in yo' weakened state. They'll take advantage of it.

You know how this game is. If you show any vulnerability to the competition, they'll exploit your weakness."

"Exactly," Fear spoke taking another swig of the Hennessy.

"Right." He coughed with a fist to his mouth. "Check it though. There's some new blood looking to enter the fold."

Fear sobered up right then, taking the bottle from his lips and looking to his comrade. He frowned.

"Who?"

"The Bluudlow Brothers."

"Bluudlow Brothers?" He raised an eyebrow.

"Yeah. And these niggaz are out here on some high power shit," Big Sexy told his right-hand man before taking a swig of his Budweiser. He wiped his mouth with the back of his hand before continuing. "They're making a sweep through all of the hoods on the East Side asking niggaz to get down with them. If they with it they set 'em out with some work, if they're not then they getting laid the fuck out, simple as that. Word is that they the ones that handled them niggaz, Bunchy and Ted. Remember how they were found off the 110 freeway in the trunk of Bunchy's car strangled and shot to death? Well," he took the time to scratch his nose with his pinky finger. "I heard they lil' crew put them murders down. Guess what they call themselves though? The Untouchables, why? 'Cause fools ain't stupid enough to lay a hand on 'em niggaz. And they beat hella murder beefs."

Fear shrugged and said, "Long as them niggaz keep that shit outta the twenties, I'm not tripping." He took a swig from the bottle of Hennessy. He focused his attention back on the burning logs but kept his ears open to his lieutenant.

"That's the thing, them boys are looking to expand their enterprise," Big Sexy said, "I ran into them cats at the Slauson Swapmeet earlier today once I sent moms off. The oldest brother, Bear, he got at me just as I was pulling outta the parking lot. He gave me his card and told me to give it to you. Said he has a business proposition he wants to present to you, so you know what that means. It's time to bring them thangs out."

Fear looked to his main man with furrowed brows. Hearing niggaz threatening to move in on the soil he was getting his money off of zapped the death of his father right out of his head. He no longer felt the grief and turmoil that the loss of his old man had brought. Nah, almost instantly he was converted back to that beast that the streets had made him. He became that nigga that could handle business with one of the slickest mouth pieces ever and pull them mothafucking triggers if need be.

"Looks like we're gonna have to spank 'em then. Damn, just when everything was quiet and niggaz could make a dolla without having to worry about The Ones swooping down on 'em." Fear shook his head and sat the bottle of Hen Dog down. "Let me see that card, Sex." He took the card from Big Sexy that Bear had given him and snatched up his cell phone. His forehead wrinkled when he saw several missed calls from Malik. His cell phone had been on silent the entire time so he hadn't heard it at all. "Fuck this bitch ass nigga want, Blood?" He sighed and opened the dial pad of his cellular. Looking from the number scrolled on the card to the numbers on his dial pad, he punched in the digits and placed the device to his ear. The line rang twice before a gruff voice answered. "What's up? Is Bear there?"

"Who dis?"

"This Fear, you gave my homeboy your number today at the Slauson, said you wanted to talk business."

For a moment there was silence and then he spoke again.

"Oh, yeahhh, I remember, me and my brother gotta business proposition we wanna run past you, Big Dawg. When is a good time for us to meet?"

"How about tomorrow night? 10 o'clock?"

"Cool. You got any place in mind?"

"Yeah, how about…" He gave him the address of the place they were to meet tomorrow night and disconnected the call.

"I know you not really finna bow down to them Bitch Boys?"

Fear shot Big Sexy a look that read as Nigga, please and then said, "Fuck I look like? You already know what time it is with me. Check it, I need you to put some calls in to them niggaz down by the way that the Bluudlow's put the muscle on. I want chu to set up a meeting so we can see how much it's worth to them to get these fools foot off their necks."

"Ohhhhhh," he said finally realizing what his boss was doing.

"Right," the hustler continued, "I can get rid of the school yard bully but why do it for free, ya Griff me?"

"Sho' ya right." The big man finished off his Budweiser and sat it down on the coffee table. "My nigga is back y'all." He smiled and dapped him up, thinking back to when he'd first met him.

*****

They were enclosed in a circle of men and women egging them on and hurling insults. The atmosphere was humid and made it harder for them to breathe, but still their fight raged on with neither of them wanting to give in. They were hot, exhausted, sweaty and thirsty, but they could not give up. They would not give up because tonight's champion was not only guaranteed two hundred dollars, but a couple hot meals and a place to crash for a couple nights. Now that may not seem like much to an Average Joe, but to two homeless men like Travis Winkle and Big Sexy, it was just as good as a winning lottery ticket for four million dollars which was why the two brutes were slugging it out with all that they had.

Bwhack! Crack! Wapp!

Travis's head whipped from left to right. The final blow sent his blood splattering against someone's face causing them to stagger backwards. He fell into the arms of the audience and they threw him back in. His face was swollen and bloody and he was breathing hard. His eyes were hooded and looking about lazily as he mustered up the strength to hold up his marred fists. The bigger man took wild swings at Big Sexy. They were rather fast but he dodged them with finesse and moved in, wreaking havoc on his body and face. Sweat and blood flew from Travis looking like diamonds and blood rubies beneath the lights inside of the room. He staggered backwards fast, turning his body halfway before crashing to the floor where specs of blood and loose teeth lay from other fighters that had fought from earlier that night.

"Ahhhhh!"

"Ahhhhh!"

"Ahhhhh!"

The audience erupted. Most of them were happy that Big Sexy had dropped old boy, but the rest were disappointed because they had dropped large sums of money on him to win. A battered and bruised Travis lay on the floor staring up at his opponent. His shoulders lifted and dropped as he breathed with his fists before his face. Only the outlining of his body was noticeable to him. The rest of him was hidden by the shadows of the room, save for his eyes which looked like two glowing red orbs. The big man resembled a beast to Travis and he was too weak to fight much more so he just laid there to receive the rest of his punishment. And that he did.

"Finish him!"

"Finish him!"

"Finish him!"

The audience gassed Big Sexy and cheered him on. He sped walked over to his distraught opponent and straddled him, beating his face with his fists. The punches sounded like he was striking a slab of raw pork ribs. Blood splattered against him with each fist that landed against the opposition's face, shifting his bone structure.

"He's done, stop, that's enough!" An old man rocking a ball head and wife beater ordered, cutting his arms across one another. Big Sexy stopped just as he was about to throw the last punch, letting his arm fall beside him. He looked down at the bloody mess that he'd created. Travis's eyes were swollen shut, his nose was broken and he was missing an entire row of front teeth. The blood that slicked his face was black and looked like an oil spill. Big Sexy placed his hand on his knee and pushed up off the floor. He nearly staggered backwards and fell, until the ref caught him. Taking his wrist, he held it high up in the air and declared him the champion. The audience applauded and cheering the bigger man. He was handed a white towel and a bottle of water. After guzzling down the water, he took the towel and wiped his face down, trekking through the crowd of onlookers. They gave him high fives and pats on the back as he passed through the sea of them.

As the audience closed behind Big Sexy two shady men emerged turning to his back as he walked away to clean up, collect his winnings, and head to his hotel room. Their faces were partially hidden by the shadows and they spoke amongst one another in hushed tones so that no one would hear what they were discussing. Both men were heated that he'd won and cost them the few hundred dollars they'd bet.

Their plan as of now was to rob him before he'd gotten the chance to spend his money. One of them tapped the other and they headed off in Big Sexy's direction. They played the shadows watching him get dressed and collect his earnings before making his exit, his backpack slung over his shoulder.

Big Sexy was walking through the parking lot between cars when suddenly one of the men appeared before him from behind a Dodge Intrepid, freezing him cold in his tracks. The man face's was hard and the gun he'd just raised promised threats of violence if he didn't get what he'd come for.

"You know what time it is, come up off all that shit, nigga, asap!" He ordered with attitude, ready to attribute to the Southern California's growing murder rate.

"I ain't even worth the bullets, G; all I got is two hundred funky ass dollas and a punk ass subway gift card."Big Sexy admitted, battered, bruised and exhausted from the brawl. All he wanted was to grab something to eat and head to his hotel.

The gunman shrugged and said, "Ain't much but we'll take it."

"You got me all of the way fucked up!" Big Sexy's eyebrows arched and his nose scrunched up.

"Either you gon' gimmie what you got, or I'ma give you what I got," he demanded. With that said, his partner in crime appeared at the back of their prey, gun extended at the back of his dome. Big Sexy's eyes shifted to their corners feeling someone at his rear. They came back around to the gunman standing before him and a devilish smile stretched across his lips, his gold capped tooth twinkled. He licked his top row of teeth and bit down on his bottom lip. "You were saying?"

Big Sexy took a deep breath and lowered his eyes, looking back up he gave him a nod which was his way of saying that he was going to comply. With lightning fast reflexes, the husky man threw his head to the left narrowly missing the bullet from the nigga at the back of him. He swung his backpack around and knocked the gun from the nigga in front of him. The banger went up into the air and came slamming down on the hood of a Pontiac Grand Am. Dude that had been holding the steel on him staggered backwards, hitting his head on the bumper of a parked Nissan Sentra and fell to the ground. He lay there groaning in pain, face wincing. The sound of a bone crackling and popping, along with a eardrum shattering scream caused Big Sexy to whip around. His brow furrowed when he saw a mysterious man in a hood, breaking the gunman's arm and twisting it up around his back. He dropped his gun and it clasped when it the ground, standing upward before falling down to the surface. The hooded man slammed his victim into the trunk of a Cadillac repeatedly before slamming it into the back window of the vehicle. The glass cracked into a spider's cobweb and left blood outlining the breakage. As soon as the stranger dropped his victim to the ground and pulled out his .9mm. Pointing his banger down at him, he pulled the trigger rapidly.

Boc! Boc! Boc! Boc!

Big Sexy was slightly startled seeing the man in the hood put in that work. He looked back around and found the gunman he'd dropped moaning in pain.

"Finish 'em." The man ordered him. "Finish 'em now." With Big Sexy not moving fast enough for him; the stranger in the hood pointed his head bussa at him. His body tensed but he quickly recovered, remembering he was a G. "Do it!"

Hesitantly, Big Sexy snatched the handgun up from off the hood of the Pontiac Grand Am and approached the sprawled man. He stepped over his backpack and stood over him, leveling his steel at his dome piece.

"Uhhhhh!" The man's moans were silenced as soon as they'd begun.

Pop! Pop! Pop! Pop! He gave his bitch ass some wings so that he could get to heaven.

The stranger popped two slugs into the already dead gunman's body. "Now put one into the mothafucka laid out behind me!" The husky man nodded and did as he was told, gunshots followed with flashes of light.

Dude in the hood tucked his piece and took a cautious scan of the area, making sure there wasn't anyone around that could have possibly seen them. He snatched the tool from Big Sexy and tucked it into the front of his jeans. Next, he grabbed him by the sleeve of his jacket and ushered him off, still looking all around to make sure no one had made them.

"Come on; let's get the fuck up outta here."He pulled him along and grabbed his backpack up, passing it off to him.

***

Big Sexy rode shotgun while dude in the hood pushed the wheel, taking cautious glances through the side view and rearview mirrors to make sure The Boys weren't following them. Once he felt safe, he relaxed and pulled the hood from off of his head. That's when Big Sexy was able to get a good look at him. He was a dark chocolate man of short stature and a body that put you in the mind of Ja Rule now that he was buff. His hair was spinning in waves and he fancied a goatee that was razor edge sharp. The illumination of the streetlight posts flickered on and off of him each time he drove under them, playing with the lighting of his face.

"What's yo' name, family?" He asked his passenger and now partner and crime.

"Big Sexy."

"Fuck you say to me?" He frowned thinking homeboy was trying to sex playing him on some homo shit.

"My name is Big Sexy." He extended his meaty hand in a friendly gestured. It lingered there a while before the stranger finally accepted it.

"People actually call a grown ass man Big Sexy?" He raised an eyebrow.

"Yep."

"I'm curious. Why in the hell do you call yo' self Big Sexy?"

"Shit, you can't tell? 'Cause I'm one big sexy mothafucka." He grinned and gave himself the once over. This caused Fear to shake his head and grin himself.

"Well, Big Sexy, I'm Fearless, but chu can just call me Fear." He gave him a firm handshake and looked him dead in the eyes. You could always tell if a nigga had been through some shit through his eyes. Off top he acknowledged that the husky man had been through hell and back. Through it all he was still standing ten toes down though, throwing back whatever life threw at him. He respected that. It showed that he wasn't for laying down and dying. He was a mothafucking soldier.

"Thanks for saving my ass back there, but where did you come from?" Big Sexy inquired.

"I watched yo' fight, I had a couple stacks betted on you." He informed him. "While I was collecting my winnings I made them two crafty ass niggaz eyeballing you so I knew they were about to make their move."

"Not that I'm not grateful, but why? You could have kept pushing. You don't owe me jack shit."

"I'ma sinner, homie, hopefully this good deed will reserve me a place in heaven." He glanced down at his lap and saw the weapons there that had been used to murder the niggaz that had tried to rob Big Sexy. "Yo' do me a favor and pop that glove box open, Big Dawg, and grab that rag outta there for me." After doing what he'd been told, he watched as Fear sat the guns inside of the rag and folded it up around them. Next, he was being handed the rag back to be placed back inside of the glove box. "Thanks." He adjusted himself in the seat, getting a little more comfortable.

"Wait, you don't plan on keeping those burners, do you?" He asked with both eyebrows raised. "Them shits got two murders on them."

"Yes, and I know," Fear answered nonchalantly. "This is the tie that binds us. This is our guarantee that no one here will rat 'cause if one burns then we all burn."

"Hold up, homie," Big Sexy turned around to him in his seat. "Are you calling me a snitch? 'Cause I ain't no mothafucking snitch."

"What I'm saying is that there's only one person in this ride that I trust. And guess who that is." He looked from him to the windshield smiling.

"Fair enough." He focused his attention outside on the streets as they flew passed him.

Fear and Big Sexy grew close afterwards. The young kingpin allowed him to come stay with him. He taught him the game and gave him the job of being his enforcer. He made a damn good one too. When niggaz was tripping or there was debt that needed to be collected, Big Sexy was sent to make an example out of a mothafucka.

He handed down extreme punishment for the minute of violations and rewarded anyone within the operation that had any information on anyone doing shady shit behind Fear's back. Once Big Sexy got done with that list of people, he chilled out and took a break to stay off the radar of police. Now here he was the lieutenant to his man's empire.

Big Sexy headed out of the door pulling it shut behind him and smiling. It felt good to know that his nigga'z head was back in the game. Now they could smash the competition and get back to getting the money.

The next day

A white on white Chevy Trail Blazer pulled upon the block and the driver executed its engine. Its occupants were The Bluudlow Brothers, Bear and Terrence; from the first glance of the siblings you wouldn't have thought that they shared the same parents. They were as different as night and day when it came to appearances. Bear was a 6 foot 3 fella with a flabby body and an almond hue. His chubby, hairy face and meaty arms gave him the appearance of a grizzly bear. Though he was a threat he was hardly the most violent of the pair. That title belonged to the shortest and oldest of them. Terrance stood 5 foot 7 easy. He had dark coal skin and a lean body that was cut and formed a V from the underarms. He was the brain of their little outfit, while Bear was the brawn. From time to time he'd let his gun come out for mischief, but he really got a kick watching his underlings wreck shit.

"So this is their lil' block, huh?" Bear asked Terrance as their eyes took in the full scope of the block. There were dope fiends coming to and from the corner to get their prescriptions filled. "This mu'fucka banging, Bro, it's money out here."

"Right," Terrance replied, "It's ripe for the picking, which is why we're here to take it all."

"Sho' ya right." Bear nodded. "Are there any particulars you need to kick about these fools?"

"None that I'm aware of but you'll do yourself a service to keep your eyes peeled," Terrance warned him.

"Remember, a fearful cat will strike out when its back is against the wall just as a feral one would."

"Bah," Bear waved him off nonchalantly, "This block wreaks of pussies."

Terrance didn't utter another word as he opened the glove-box and retrieved the packaged that was inside. He tucked it inside of his jacket and he and Bear hopped out. Once he secured his .9mm in the small of his back. He adjusted his glasses and he and Bear jogged across the street. The two moved easily up the sidewalk brushing shoulders with dope fiends that had just got their medication and were off to take their first dose.

"Yo, young boy, can I get a moment of your time?" Terrance asked as he and Bear approached.

The youth that was serving the fiends turned around chewing on a straw. He was sporting a Milwaukee Bucks jersey and camouflage cargo pants.

"Time is money, my nigga, and I don't have a dolla to waste." He held up his G-shock watch and tapped his finger against its glass face.

"I'm only looking for a minute or two, nothing more, nothing less." Terrance assured him and placed his hand to his chest. "I'm here on a humble."

"Walk nigga, I'm on a come up." Milwaukee jersey turned away from Terrance and went back to serving the fiends bopping through.

"My man," Bear lifted his shirt and exposed the twin revolvers resting in his waistline. When he'd called Milwaukee jersey, the youngster turned around ready to buck but seeing the weapons changed his attitude. "My brother requested a few ticks; I suggest you entertain his conversation 'fore you see the interior of a coffin."

Fear froze Milwaukee jersey's heart and he swallowed the lump in his throat. Knowing that a couple of hollow points would be detrimental to his health he nodded and agreed to chop it up with the oldest Bluudlow brother.

"What's your name, homie?" Terrance asked.

"Roscoe."

"Is this your block, Roscoe?"

"Nah," he shook his head.

"Well, present me to the man in charge of this dog and pony show."

Roscoe nodded and looked over his shoulder. Sticking his pinky fingers on each side of his mouth, he whistled and waved the man in charge over. The cat Terrance and Bear were looking for was named, D-Block. At the time he was hunched over inside the drive side window of a burgundy Honda Accord hollering at what he hoped would be his future baby momma. When Roscoe called D-Block, he wrapped up the conversation with home girl in the Honda and headed in his direction.

"What's up?" D-Block threw his head back.

"These dudes wanted to holla at chu," Roscoe told him.

D-Block looked Bear and Terrance up and down and sighed. Their presence disgusted him, seeing them was like finding dog shit on the heel of his sneaker. "I know y'all niggaz, fam?"

"Is this your block?" Terrance asked.

"Who wants to know?"

Terrance looked to Bear and gave him a nod. Swiftly, the giant raised his tool and pulled the trigger. D-Block's head came apart and sent chunks of flesh and brain fragments everywhere. Red goo splattered against the side of Roscoe's face and specs of it clung to the lenses of Terrance's glasses. The loud bang of the gun sent the people in the area scattering like frightened mice. Bear's eyes shifted to the left and saw the brim of a Red Sox cap creeping along the side of a parked Nissan Sentra trying to get the drop on him. Extending his weapon in that direction, Bear waited for his target to spring out to take a shot and when he did, he gave him three searing hot slugs to the chest. The boy fell in what looked like slow motion before lying flat in the street.

"You," Bear hollered to a youth across the street wearing a beanie. He looked like he was deciding whether he should run or not. "Don't even try to run, my nigga, I got four more left in this revolver and I bet they'll make it to the end of the block before you do. Bring that ass on." He motioned the youth over with a wave of his revolver. Reluctantly, the youth came across the street and stood beside Roscoe.

Terrance removed his glasses and pulled a cloth from his back pocket. Using the cloth, he rubbed out the specs of blood on the lenses of his glasses. He then fogged the lenses with his breath and repeated this until the lenses were free of red smears. He then slipped the glasses back on and looked up at the young men before him. Roscoe was trembling and his teeth were chattering, while the other kid looked as if he was silently praying to God Almighty.

"Now," Terrance began, "What are y'all pumping out here?"

"P—Pa—Panic," Roscoe managed to get out.

"Gimmie what chu got left." Terrance opened his palm.

Roscoe reached inside of the gutter and pulled out a greasy brown paper bag. He removed the cup that was inside, took off the lid and dumped ten packets labeled Panic into Terrance's palm. Terrance looked down at his palm and then back up at Roscoe.

"Is that it?"

"Yeah, man, that's it, I swear to God."

"Good." When Terrance went to pull something from his back the young men tensed. "Easy now, I gotta lil' something for ya." He pulled the package from his back and tossed it to Roscoe. Roscoe hurriedly opened the package. Inside were about three hundred packets labeled Headache.

"From now on, this block belongs to The Bluudlow Brothers," Terrance told them. "If I come 'round here and I see anything pumping out besides Headache, y'all lil' niggaz gone see red. Straight up, do we understand each other?"

The young men nodded in unison.

"I'ma hit y'all with a package like that at the end of every week. That's every Friday," Terrance informed them. "You lil' niggaz be out here at 6 A.M every Friday. What's ya count?" he asked the youth in the beanie.

Beanie pulled out the money and shuffled through the bills.

"I gotta G-Ball," He reported.

Terrance snatched the money from him and relieved D-Block of whatever cash he had on him. He quickly counted the money and came up with a total of $2400 dollars. He gave the young men $1200 dollars apiece. Having the money made a slight smirk appear on their faces.

"That's a stimulus," Terrance told them. "I'ma hit y'all with six hunnit a week."

The young men were ecstatic. Shit, D-Block was only giving them four hundred a week. With a two hundred dollar increase, they felt like they'd hit The Lottery.

"Y'all lil niggaz gone and beat the blade, man. One Time is on the way," Bear ordered and the young men ran from off the block. Casually, The Bluudlow Brothers made their way back to their truck.

"What did I tell ya, bro? Pussies," Bear relayed to Terrance.

CHAPTER EIGHT
2010
That night

Fear's meeting with the cats that The Bluudlow Brothers had put the muscle on took place that same night at Club Mack Daddy. Old Man Rydell masqueraded as the sole owner of the joint but Fear was a silent partner. The place had almost shut down last year until Fear approached the old man with a proposition. He'd step in as his silent partner splitting everything fifty, fifty in exchange for the hundred grand he'd give him to save the club. Old Man Rydell agreed because he knew that if the doors closed on the place, his heart would stop soon after. He loved that establishment almost as much as he loved his three teenage girls.

Fear sat in Old Man Rydell's office leant back in the executive chair with his hands nestled in his lap and his sneakers propped upon the long, cherry wood table. The walls of the office pulsated from the loud music down stairs; Eminem's Bitch Please II was pumping through the speakers. Fear leaned forth and picked up his glass of cranberry and Vodka. He'd just taken a sip when Big Sexy came through the office door and held it open for their guests. One by one, ten men filed across the threshold and took a seat at the long, cherry wood table. Before them sat glasses of water with slices of lemon on their rims and at the center of the table sat a pitcher of ice water with slices of lemon floating on the surface.

"I called you all here today because we all have a common enemy," Fear began, "An enemy that I am more than capable of ridding us all of, but it's not gonna come cheap. You mothafuckaz are gonna have to kick in."

"Who are we talking about here?" Stony spoke up.

"The Bluudlow Brothers, unless you niggaz got some mo' niggaz in yo' pockets," Fear looked around at all of the faces seated around the table. "I didn't think so. Like I was saying, before I was so rudely interrupted," he shot Stony a dangerous look, "I can take care of The Bluudlow Brothers for y'all, but it's gonna cost ya a lil' something."

"How much are we talking?" Fruity asked from the far end of the table.

"Good question, Fruity," Fear massaged his chin as he walked around the table. "A million dollars, y'all gimmie a mill and I'll make all this bullshit y'all been going through these past few months seem like a bad dream."

"I don't know, man, that seems like a tall order." Mo Mo said.

"Nigga, please, that shit is peanuts spread throughout the ten of you niggaz." Fear frowned and twisted his lips. "I should be asking for more than that seeing as how these cock suckaz have been such a thorn in your sides. You either break mine off or keep those Kibbles & Bits them dudes leave y'all with every week. You gotta 'bout ten seconds to make your decision, after that y'all can bounce your asses up outta here." He put his fingers tips together and watched as the ten men whispered amongst each other. It took about five seconds for them to deliberate.

Suddenly, silence fell on the ten men and the oldest and wisest of them, Benzo, rose to his feet and buttoned his suit. He cleared his throat before speaking in a dry, raspy voice.

"All right, young blood, you've got yourself a play," Benzo began and lifted a finger, "One million dollars for The Bluudlow Brothers."

"All right, I want that paper tomorrow at noon, gentlemen, and notta minute after. Do we understand one another?" Fear looked around at all of them; they all nodded in agreement. "Good. Dismissed." He swung back around in the executive's chair, leaving the ten men with his back as they headed out of the office.

Once everyone had gone, Big Sexy closed the office door and sat down on the cherry wood table. At this time, Fear swung back around in the executive's chair. He and Big Sexy stared at one another wearing serious expressions until they busted up laughing and smiling. They slapped hands and snapped their fingers.

"Yo, dawg, this is gonna be the easiest mill we've ever made." Big Sexy said.

"Yeah, I should have charged their punk asses twice that for being such pansies." Fear shook his head. "I can't believe them brothers got these niggaz shaking like they work at The Barbie Coast. I should have muscled my way onto their territory and put my product out there."

"Shit, fam, it ain't too late, fuck them niggaz." Big Sexy said. "You know me, I'm all for the betterment of the team; run with us or run from us. That's my motto."

"Nah, I don't want to be greedy about the shit," Fear admitted. "I'ma just play the cards I was dealt. If I don't like this hand, I'll just put the stainless to the dealer's head and make him reshuffle the deck."

Night turned into today as if by magic. Before Fear knew what was going on, it was noon and the cat that was supposed to be delivering the million dollars came waltzing into Old Man Rydell's office. The fellow sat the briefcase down before Fear and sat down beside him. Fear popped the locks on the briefcase and raised the lid. The sound of a cash register went off in his head Cha-Ching! He leaned over into the brief case, closing his eyes and inhaling the scent of the big face hundred dollar bills. Fear lay back in his seat with a smile plastered on his face. He lit up an L and as he took a puff he fanned out the match he'd used to light it.

"Big, you locked that door, my nigga?" Fear asked Big Sexy who was standing by the door gripping a KG-9. He nodded his answer. "Good," he looked to the cat that brought the money. "This is a million dollars, right?" the cat nodded. "Big, if this briefcase is a dollar short of a million, I want chu to put a hole through this nigga's head."

"Roger that," Big Sexy replied.

Just then, the cat reached inside of his jacket and pulled out a brick of money. He smacked it down on the table and Fear snatched it up.

"Youz a filthy mothafucka," Fear shook his head and then looked to Big Sexy. "You believe this shit? You can't trust anyone these days."

"Tell me about it," Big Sexy said.

Out of the blue, Fear struck the cat across the face with the brick of money. The impact was so great that it sent the chair hurtling backwards and the cat spilling out of it. Fear straddled him and began beating his face with the brick of money. Once he was done, he got to his feet, breathing hard and looking at the brick of money; it had specks of blood on it. Fear looked to the cat he'd thrown the beating to. He lay on the floor twitching and moaning in pain. The cat's face was coated red. His left eye was swollen shut and his grill was busted up.

As if nothing had occurred, Fear sat back down in his chair and pulled it closer to the table. He then began running the money from the briefcase through a money-counter as he casually smoked the L. Finishing the count, Fear locked the briefcase back and picked it up from off the table. He looked over to Big Sexy and said, "Come on, I need to put this loot up."

"What about cha man." Big Sexy nodded to the bloodied cat lying on the floor.

"Fuck 'em," Fear answered. "Let his misery keep 'em company."

Darkness enveloped the sky and with it came the cold, crisp air of the night. It was 9: 58 P.M and Fear was posted up in front of a garage of an old abandoned house on a dead end street. He smoked on a smoldering cigarette as he waited for The Bluudlow Brothers to arrive. For the fifth time that night he glanced at his Movado watch. The clock had just struck 10 o'clock on the dot. He was caught off guard by the approaching headlights and the purr of an engine as a truck headed in his direction. Fear didn't have to wonder who it was because the license plate gave them away Bluudlow. The truck pulled up alongside the curb and The Bluudlow Brothers hopped out. They took in the scope of their surroundings as they approached Fear. The men exchanged pleasantries before they presented Fear with their business proposition.

"Thanks but no thanks, fellas," Fear told the brothers after hearing their proposal.

"You sure about this, fam?" Bear gave him a look that said You really need to take this offer.

"Positive," Fear answered. "I'm running my own show. It doesn't make since for me to demote myself for a slice of the pie that's significantly smaller."

"I heard that. Well we're in the wind." Terrance gave Fear dap and he and Bear headed back to the truck. Bear pulled his heater and turned back around to Fear. He went to pull the trigger of his weapon at the same Fear was firing up a cigarette. Bear was none the wiser of that being the signal. He never knew what hit him.

Choot!

Bear's eyes bulged as a red mist sprayed from the side of his neck. He gagged and choked trying to stop the bleeding by applying pressure to the wound with his hand. He staggered forth like a Zombie but eventually collapsed. Gun at the ready, Terrance's head snapped from left to right trying to see were the ghetto sniper's bullets came from. Not able to see anyone in the darkness, he looked to where Fear was standing and he'd vanished. Hearing rustling at his rear, Terrance swung his gun around ready to make a nigga'z momma cry. When he didn't see anyone behind him, he anticipated a bullet striking him. He just didn't know where it would come from.

A sizzling bullet whizzed through Terrance's left cheek tearing through gum and teeth. He howled in agony feeling the ember shred his flesh. He fell on his side still gripping his banger and wailing in excruciation. Big Sexy emerged from out of the shadows dressed in a black beanie cap pulled low over his brows and a black bandana that covered the lower half of his face. His attire was black army fatigues and matching combat boots. His movements were so fluid that you wouldn't think he was 200 and something odd pounds. Big Sexy didn't waste any time staking claim on the lives laid before his feet. With the grace of a ballerina he swept in on Bear and gave him two to his cabbage. Next in line was Terrance, the oldest of The Bluudlow Brothers ,managed to hold up the middle finger at his enemy and flash a smile. The giant smiled evilly at him before shooting off his middle finger.

"Arrhhh!" He hollered in agony but several more of those hollow points to the chest shut him up forever.

Choot! Choot! Choot! Choot! Choot!

After finishing off The Bluudlow Brothers, Big Sexy looked up and saw Fear approaching with a machete. He grabbed Terrance by the ankle and dragged him back towards to the garage before hustling back over.

"What're you doing?" Big Sexy asked.

"Making a statement," Fear answered. "Now help me drag this fat piece of shit back towards the garage."

Big Sexy helped Fear drag Bear's corpse in front of the garage. Fear took a couple more puffs from his cigarette before passing it to Big Sexy and going to work on the bodies with his machete. The next morning the police would find The Bluudlow Brothers in front of the garage with their severed heads sitting on their backs. Written on the garage door in blood was a message: Anybody can get it.

A few days later

It had taken longer than he'd expected, but Fear was finally able to make his way inside of the visiting room of the state prison. He traveled along the row of loved ones sitting on the stools waiting to see the person for their reason of making such a long journey. Once he found the stool he was supposed to sit to wait on who he'd come to pay a call upon, he sat down and folded his arms across his chest, tapping his Timb impatiently.

He looked through the Plexiglas as the inmates walked through the visiting room door, all of them wearing sky blue button-down shirts with C.D.C on the backs of them and navy blues pants. First came a Mexican with a face covered in tattoos, then came a Native American man, then there was a young, skinny white dude, a portly brotha, and lastly, Malik. He wore a hard face that complimented his new muscular build. His thick beard was untamed while the hair on head had grown considerably longer, showing signs of graying from the stress of a life sentence. His hair was parted down the middle and braided into two lengthy pigtails that lay over his shoulders. The last of the inmates that had entered the visiting room along with him had all just crossed Fear's line of vision, when his cousin drew up his pants before sitting down before him. For a time they just sat there still studying one another. Their eyes lifeless, their faces void of emotion.

Keeping his eyes on his relative, Fear picked up the telephone slowly and stopped it at midpoint to his ear. He stared at his cousin because if he wasn't about to pick up the telephone on his side of the patrician then he was about to hang up. Suddenly, Malik picked up the telephone and placed it to his ear. He didn't say a word as he stared down his visitor, nostrils throbbing and jaws pulsating. His eyes became glassy and red webbed. He was heated, on one.

"What up, G? Aint chu gon' say something."

"Fuck you won't, nigga?" He spat so hard that his spittle went flying from his lips, splattering against the thick glass. Looking over Malik's shoulder, Fear saw two C.Os move closer just in case his kin popped off. After peeping the move, he settle back on the person he'd come to see. He was unnerved by the display of aggression and he went on talking like everything was cool and calm.

"I can't come and check on my peoples? Damn!" He said like It's like that now, homie? "I heard about what happened to Wameek, dawg, that's fucked up." Pinching the beginning of his nose, he shook his head regretfully. Next, he looked back up with serious and glassy eyes.

***

Wearing a tear streak face, Wameek tied a length of sheets and blankets together. Once his creation was done, he tied it around his neck and tugged on it, testing its restraint. Satisfied he stepped to the mirror inside of his cell. Whimpering and sniffling, he said a prayer and kissed the crucifix around his neck. On the verge of breaking down, he shuddered and wiped his wet cheeks with the back of his hand. With that out of the way, he walked out of his housing unit and climbed upon the guard railing. He outstretched his arms and widened the gap between his legs, trying to keep his balance as he looked down. A gathering of cons quickly formed, looking up at him and cheering him on to jump, pumping their fists. Right then he heard the panic alarm blaring loud and without remorse. He looked up and down the tier and saw C.Os running toward him from both directions, en route to stop his suicide attempt.

"Jump! Jump! Jump!" he heard the words of encouragement below. Some of these men were lifers to and tired of living their lives behind bars. They only wished that they had the balls to do what Wameek was about to do.

Wameek took two deep breaths, shut his eyes and said, "Father, forgive me..." When he looked back down the men were still below him egging him on. He swallowed the lump of nervousness that had formed inside of his throat. Closing his eyes, he threw his head back and crossed himself in the sign of the crucifix before jumping. His arms waved wildly and his legs kicked a little. Looking below him, it appeared as if the ground was flying toward him, but in actuality he was falling toward it.

"Yuuuck!" the chain of sheets and blankets snatched his ass back up before he could hit the ground. He clutched at the homemade noose around his neck, eyes bulging and webbing red, his legs kicking wildly. Darkness expanded at the crotch of his pants and yellow droplets rained beneath him. The inmates stared up at him in shock; eyes wide and slacked jawed at his dancing from the rope.

Present

"You know for as gangsta as that nigga was and as much shit that we've done in the streets, I thought that cho baby bro would have held his head and done his time like a mothafucking man. But when reality struck that he was gon' spend the rest of his natural life in this here shithole, all of the bitch came bleeding up outta that nigga." Fear took the time to gather his thoughts before continuing. "Hmmph, this whole time that nigga was wearing a thong underneath them Dickies." When he said this, Malik's eyes ran with tears and his top lip twitched with anger. Fear had looked away shaking his head and massaging his chin. Truthfully, he was fucked up behind Wameek's actions. They may have not seen eye to eye, but he did respect his gangsta. But now that respect was gone and he looked at him like he was pathetic.

Seeing that he'd gotten to Malik, Fear decided to torment him further. He casted his eyes back in his direction. "You know, I can't help to think since his lil' punk ass molded his G after you, could it be possible that big bro is just as big of a pussy as his lil' bro?" He smiled evilly and licked his top row of teeth, knowing that his words would strike a nerve.

"Fuck you! Fuck you! Fuck you!" Malik roared, his spittle smacking up against the Plexiglas and running like beads of sweat. His actions startled the visitors as well as the other cons inside of the facility. They jumped back or looked his way with lines formed across their foreheads. Furious, he threw the telephone at the glass causing it to make a Ding sound when it deflected. "Bitch made ass nigga, I'll rip yo' fuckin' heart out, you fuckin' Judas!" He kicked and kicked the partition that separated them with rage, destined to break it and get to him. Fear just sat there laughing his ass off. He wasn't the least bit afraid of his cousin. That ass wasn't ever getting out and even if he did, so fucking what. He was with the shit so murder wasn't a thang for him. The C.Os rushed in and Malik succeeded in knocking one of them out, but the second clocked him over the head. He winced but kept throwing them hands. Before he knew it, he was fighting with the both of them. While he was chunking them with the correction officers, Fear stood up and walked away. His back was to them as he casually strolled away laughing like he'd heard the funniest joke in the world.

With The Bluudlow Brothers out of the way, Fear moved forward to dismantle The Untouchables.

CHAPTER NINE
2003

It was a beautiful Wednesday morning. The birds were chirping and the rays of the warm sun were peeking through the chocolate blinds of Black Jesus' bedroom. The El Salvadorian drug lord lied peacefully asleep in his king-size bed under his soft Egyptian cotton sheets. Suddenly his bed rocked back and forth from someone jumping up and down in it. The peaceful look of sleep on Black Jesus' face gave way to a frown. His eyes fluttered open and he turned over in bed, wiping the morning scum from his eyes.

"Wake up, mothafucka! Those two crazy mothafuckaz did it!"

Black Jesus' vision comes into focus and he sees Bullet in his wife beater and boxers jumping up and down in his bed.

"What's your malfunction, cabrone?" Black Jesus said, groggily. "Jumping around in my bed like you're five years old. I should kick your little brown ass."

"Sure later," Lethal said nonchalantly. "But check this out first." He flopped down on the bed and clicked on the 50" flat-screen. He then flipped through the channels until he found Channel 5 News. There was a news report on about the murders of Police Sergeant Daniel O'Connor and his family.

"I told you those two would pull it off," Gustavo said behind a radiant smile. He sat up in bed and nestled his bare feet in the mink carpet.

There was a knock on the doorway of the bedroom which drew the drug lord's attention. When he turned around, he saw that it was Broomhilda.

"Good morning, Mr. Sanchez. I hope I am not interrupting anything. But you have visitors; Senor Malik,

Wameek and Fear are here to see you," She informed him timidly.

"Where are they?" He slipped on his robe and tied it around his waist.

"They're in the living room, sir."

"Offer them something to eat and drink. I'll be with them shortly." He stuck in his feet into a pair of slippers.

"Si," she nodded before leaving the room.

After showering, shaving and brushing his teeth, the drug lord got dressed and hopped upon his Segway motorized scooter. He rolled down the hallway and into the living room where he found Lethal and the cousins waiting for him. Once he stepped off of the scooter, he greeted the men with firm handshakes like he'd done in their initial meeting. Lethal mad dogged them as his boss gave them props for taking out Sergeant O'Connor, but expressed his displeasure of them murdering their children. Still, Gustavo Sanchez was a man that was all about business and he understood the casualties that came with getting certain jobs done. The execution of the kids was a stain on his soul that he'd have to live with. When it came to getting Black Jesus' revenge, it was a small price to pay.

Malik explained to the drug lord his disappointment with the sergeant's kids getting the business. He understood his people's reasoning behind slaughtering the twins. That was only because his brother had told him that his cover was blown and he had to do what he had to do. Fear had backed up the lie to keep the bullshit down and avoid his older cousin's scolding. He wasn't trying to hear that shit. The young nigga had enough on his mind with the four murders. Malik understood that what was done couldn't be reverse. He knew that God would frown upon the heinous act they all were involved in, but was confident that with all the paper he was about to make with his new plug, he was going to have enough loot to buy his way into heaven.

"This is for you," Fear handed Gustavo a gift wrapped box. It was pretty heavy. He shook it a little and placed his ear to it, listening to see if he'd hear a ticking noise. For all he knew, he'd been handed him a time-bomb. "What chu you doing, family? Gon' and open it." He laughed.

Gustavo chuckled and said, "I've made quite a number of enemies over the years. You can never be too careful." He tore off the wrapping and let the paper drop to the floor before opening the box. He reached inside and produced a bronzed human head, Police Sergeant Daniel O'Connor's head. The drug lord looked to the short killer and cracked a smile. Right after, he extended the head before him and looked straight into its face.

"I guess my birthday came early," he chuckled, happy with his present. "I'll assume that this was your handiwork?"

"No doubt." Fear replied with a nod, sitting upon the couch.

"What's your name again, kid?" He inquired.

Fear was quiet for a time, thinking on it before he replied. He looked up from the floor where his eyes had been focused.

"Fearless, but chu can call me Fear."

"Hmmm, Fearless, I like that. I like that a lot." Having placed the bronze head on the living room table, he clipped the end of a fresh cigar. "Now as for business." He took a couple of puffs from the overgrown cancer stick, creating smoke clouds.

"Right, business," Malik spoke up, smacking his hands and rubbing them together. He placed a silver briefcase on his lap and popped the locks. "I'll take fifty kilos."

Gustavo whistled at the thought of fifty bricks of cocaine, taking a healthy pull from his cigar. "That's a lot of cocaine, my friend." He blew smoke into the air, adding to the fog around them. "You sure you can move that much blow?"

"Is a pig's pussy pork?" Malik responded confidently.

"Confidence, one can never have too much." The drug lord nodded before casting his eyes on Malik. He nodded his head to a beat inside of his head and drummed his fingers in a rhythm on the silver briefcase. "Okay, hustle-man. You cop fifteen keys from me, and I'll front you the other fifteen on consignment, how's that sound?"

"Fuck a consignment! That's for niggaz with short paper," Malik exclaimed, talking like he was already Top Dawg. "I'm copping all of mine up front." He popped the locks on his briefcase, raised the lid, and turned it around to the drug lord and his muscle. "That's 450k."

"Malik," Gustavo began with a smile, "You never cease to amaze me."

He took a pull from the cigar and then blew out a roar of smoke.

"How many trap houses did y'all stick up to get cho hands on that kind of loot?" Lethal asked, folding his arms across his chest. "I know you mothafuckaz ain't holding like that."

"We ain't rob shit, homeboy. This money was owed to us and we collected, you nosey chinky eyed bastard." Malik frowned, not feeling homeboy coming at him like he was some broke ass nigga. Lethal's face balled up and he moved to address the unruly twin physically, but Wameek and Fear stepping to him slowed his roll. The cousins stared the man down so hard it seemed as if he would burst into flames.

Gustavo looked Malik dead in his eyes. He saw something in them that assured him that he was telling the truth.

"No, I believe him, the money is his," he informed Lethal.

He was right; Malik was indeed telling the truth. The $450,000 dollars was his and Wameek's, though. The money came from the life insurance policies of their deceased parents and sister. The boys couldn't touch a red cent of that money until they turned twenty three and here they were. One year later.

Lethal closed the silver briefcase, locked it and took it off of Malik's lap by its handle. He then turned to his boss. "I'ma take this to the back and run it through the counter," he told him before making a beeline out of the living room.

After he left, Gustavo withdrew a small flip cell phone from his robe's pocket. "Thirty, right?" he asked Malik, referring to the amount of kilos he wanted.

"Yeah, thirty," he nodded.

The drug lord was on the phone for about three minutes spewing codes in Spanish. The cousins couldn't make out a word he was saying since they weren't bilingual. But they did know what the last word meant he said into the cell phone before hanging up, gracias.

"Alright, gentlemen," Gustavo addressed the cousins, flipping the cellular shut. "You'll receive your merchandise from Merango's two trucking service on 51st and Denker Avenue; ask for Luis. There'll be a '67 Ford Mustang hooked to one of the trucks there. You'll take the truck to wherever you plan on unloading your cargo and then you'll drop it back off at the tow truck service in the morning. From there ,Luis will contact me letting me know that everything went as planned, comprende?"

"Yeah, we got it," Malik answered, motioning for his relatives to follow him as he proceeded for the door.

An hour and a half later

Fear found himself paired back up with Wameek on their way to Merango's tow truck service. As soon as they walked through the doors of the business they were greeted by Luis. The short, tubby grease monkey handed over two navy blue Dickie suits with the name of the tow truck company and their aliases, Jason and Vincent, sewn on them. He tossed Fear a key that had a pink bunny rabbit's foot attached to it and showed him the tow truck he was to take.

Fear and Wameek disrobed and stepped into the navy blue Dickie suits. He slid over into the passenger seat while his younger cousin took the wheel. He resurrected the old hog, pulled out into the street, and hopped on the freeway. He took the 105 west to the 110 east.

"They done fucked up now, reli," Wameek smiled from the front passenger seat, arm resting on the windowsill. "They gave three of the coldest niggaz outta The Bottoms the sweetest work." He took the time to light up a Kush blunt and blew a cloud of smoke into the air. "Sheiiit, we don't even have to hustle this shit. The product will sell its self." He passed the blunt to his relative, who took a few pulls and passed it back.

"Yeah, that's the best part," Fear responded holding the smoke in his lungs before he polluted the air with it.

"Yeah, once we stretch it, we gone…"

"We're not putting no cut on this shit! That's a bad idea." Fear snapped, cutting him short. From the look on his face and his body language you would have thought his kin disrespected his set.

"Man, bruh bruh already said how we gon' rock this so relax." He frowned.

"We gotta play this shit smart, family, everybody in the hood slanging some bullshit," Fear spoke his piece of mind. "If we hit these fiends with that pure they gon' be running to us. We'll be them niggaz that known out here for that premo work, ya Griff me?"

"Look, fuck what chu talking about," Wameek began. "If big bro says we stretching it then we're stretching it. I don't know what the fuck you on, but I'm on this money.

See, a nigga like me tryna squeeze every dolla he can outta this game, ya Griff me?"

"I Griff you, on mommas." Fear nodded his understanding only to get his muscle head ass to shut the fuck up. He was going to make sure he hollered at Malik to see if he could persuade him.

"Ah, shit!" Wameek blurted and sat up in his seat.

"What?" Fear asked concerned, forehead indenting.

"Binem." Wameek exclaimed, looking in the rearview mirror at a trailing police car. The sight of the black & white squad car made his stomach twist into knots. He and Fear were riding the freeway with enough work to guarantee that they would never see another sunrise again.

"Ah, fuck!" Fear cursed, after taking a peek through the rearview mirror. "Alright, okay," he inhaled and exhaled trying to calm himself. "This pig probably ain't even following us. That's it. This weed just got me tripping." He told himself and then he heard the sirens.

Blurp! Blurp! Blurp!

"Pull over onto the shoulder," A voice commanded over the loud speaker of the police cruiser.

Wameek mashed the Kush blunt out in the ashtray and let the window all of the way down, fanning the smoke out of the window.

Fear slumped down in his seat, hit his right turning signal and pulled over onto the shoulder of the freeway. He watched from his side view mirror as a muscular African American cop oozed from his vehicle and made his way in their direction sheathing a nightstick on his hip. The cop sported a bald head and a body covered in muscles, which made his uniform fit snuggly. It was a hot ass day so as soon as he stepped out of his air conditioned whip the sweat started in on him. He found himself wiping his forehead with the back of his hand as he advanced on the tow truck.

"Alright, Wa, we going to play it cool," Fear said, gripping the steering wheel and peering out of the side view mirror. "You just follow my led." He looked over to Wameek, who was still staring up at the cop through the rearview mirror.

"Nah, fuck that!" Wameek spat, resting his hand over the handle of the Beretta tucked in his pants. "Get ready to floor it cause as soon as fat boy makes it over here, I'm a leave his shit on this highway."

"Nah, Blood, play it cool," Fear whispered, seeing the officer almost at his window. Wameek was about to pull his head bussa and start dumping until he grabbed him by his wrist firmly. "I told yo' ass to be cool, nigga, so be cool." He frowned and gritted. "I got this." He released Wameek's wrist and turned to the window. The hot headed cousin threw his shirt over his burner and tried to act natural.

The cop appeared in Fear's window, smacking on gum. The short killer couldn't see his eyes through his shades so he couldn't read him. All he noticed about him was how his jaws moved like a horses eating hay as he chewed gum. The name on his shiny silver shield read, Broli.

Chewing his gum, the officer lowered his shades so that his eyes were just peeking over them. He looked from each of the cousins, and then back again before pushing his shades back upon his nose. Right after, he rested his muscular, veined arms on the windowsill and cleared his throat before speaking. Unbeknownst to him, he was making Wameek nervous. The off kilter nigga'z hand found its self inching towards that steel tucked his pants.

"Tell me, Big Dawg," Broli began. "Is that a '67 or a '68 you got hooked to the back of this here tow truck?"

Wameek let out a sigh of relief and wiped the sweat from his brows. Fear was relieved as well but he couldn't afford to let it show. He still had to put on a show for the officer.

"Oh, it's a '67, sir," Fear replied with a smile. "I see that you're a man that knows his cars."

"You bet your ass, son," The burly cop retorted. "I'm a collector. Listen, you think you could put me in touch with the owner of that there fine vehicle? I sure would like to try and buy it off of 'em."

"Sure, would you happen to have a number I could give to him to contact you?"

"I sure do," The masculine cop replied, whipping out an ink pen and a piece of paper.

For the next thirty minutes Fear and the cop traded car knowledge. The youngster knew a lot about cars because they use to help his father and grandfather work on them at his auto shop when he was kid. Every car you could think of rolled through Simpson & Son Auto Shop.

The cop let Fear go with a promise that he'd put him touch with the owner of the Mustang. The short killer gave the officer his word, the two of them shook hands and the cousins found themselves back on their way to the hood with fifty kilos of cocaine.

After dropping the tow truck back off at Merango's tow truck service, Fear, Malik and Wameek sat around the kitchen table, rotating a Kush blunt around them, the atmosphere wafting with weed smoke making the space look like the scene after an explosion.

"I was thinkin'," Malik began, passing the blunt off to Fear. "We've got all this work; we're going to need a crew to move it."

"Sho' nuff," Fear took a pull of the L and then blew smoke, clouding the air. "We gotta couple of soldiers but not enough for all of the shit we got on deck."

"I agree." Wameek nodded, agreeing with Fear.

"I got some young niggaz I been wantin' to introduce to the game," Malik claimed, pulling out his cellular. He speed dialed a particular knucklehead that he knew would bring in all the young able bodies that he needed. "We can put our own crew together. A squad of hustlas and killers to hold this empire we're about to build down, you Griff me?" He took a few pulls of the blunt.

An hour later

Fear and Wameek stood aside as Malik stood beside the raggedy stove inside of the trap house. Sitting at the kitchen table and standing around were the teenagers collected to pump the work they'd just gotten from Gustavo. The boys ranged from ages fourteen to seventeen. Although Fear didn't agree with bringing in kids this young to work for them, Malik insisted. Reasoning that if they were to ever get caught that they were looking at a hell of a lighter sentence than a grown ass man would, even if said person was a first time offender.

All of the youngsters were eating McDonalds. They were either stuffing their faces with fries, McDoubles, apple pies or slurping shakes. Even so the way they were all paying close attention to Malik made them appear as a class of Pre-K students listening to their teacher read them a story.

"It ain't no hell of a science when it comes to turning coke to crack. Really it's quite, easy." Malik sat his coffee pot of water and cocaine on one of the burners of the stove and adjusted the dial, making the blue flames erupt. "Now we sit back and watch this shit do what it do for like five minutes." He glanced at his red G-shock watch. He and the juveniles watched as white smoke manifested inside of the coffee pot, fogging it up. "See that? Now it's time for the ice." He grabbed an ice tray out of the refrigerator and got out a few ice cubes. Once he picked the coffee pot back up, he dumped the ice into it and rotated it counter clockwise, adding additional cubes when needed. "The ice is to reduce the temperature; you don't want the coke getting all fucked up." He told them. When Fear looked around at all the faces of the juveniles, they were all focused on his big cousin. They were all dying to get out in those streets and make some money. Wameek grinned noticing too. He was playing the background in the far left side of kitchen, perched backwards in a chair.

"Alright, my lil' niggaz," Malik turned around to them, still rotating the coffee pot. "She's starting to turn into a beauty. Y'all see that right there?" He pointed to the rock at the bottom of the pot succumbing to a harder substance. 'Uh huh,' the youngsters nodded their answer. He then walked over to the kitchen sink and turned the faucet on, adding cold water to the recipe. Once the coke had frozen to a solid rock, he scooped it out and sat it down on a plate. After letting the crack cool off, he slipped on some latex gloves and grabbed a box of Gemstar razors, showing the boys how to cut the shit up. He then allowed a couple of them to give him a demonstration on what he'd just taught them. A smile spread across his lips as he was pleased with all of them. He stood up clapping his hands and nodding to the rest of the outfit for them to applaud their peers as well. Next, he motioned for them to sit down and walked over so that he'd be standing to face them.

"Now that we'll gotten that shit outta the way, whose tryna make some money?" He smiled sinisterly, his head moving back and forth across the faces of the teenagers who all hand their hands raised.

"Oh, me, me, me!" one of them said.

"I wanna make some money," another chimed in.

"Pick me, Malik, man, I been tryna fuck witchu way before all of these niggaz!" a third one claimed.

Malik didn't respond to any of them. He just kept right along smiling, looking from Wameek and Fear and garnering nods of approval. Next, he took the center floor inside of the kitchen and gave an amazing speech. He sold his audience a dream, a dream only he could make come true. He promised them more money than they could ever make hustling on their own if they came to work for him. They bought the tickets that he was trying to sell. They believed in him, his dream, and most importantly, his impeccable hustling skills. Everyone in the hood knew that he was a go getter, the type of mothafucka that could make a dollar out of fifteen cents. They knew the nigga was going somewhere and they wanted seats on the train he was taking to get there.

The kitchen erupted into applause every so often during Malik's speech. By the time he had finished, he had those present eating out of the palm of his hand. Each youngling in attendance swore he was going to go harder and bring in more money than the next. Malik smiled because this was exactly what he wanted; a friendly competition amongst hustlers. By the time they entered summer he'd be swimming in a pool full of cash like Scrooge McDuck.

Malik combine the youngsters with the older heads and created what he liked to call The Cream Team, since they all were about getting money. His squad's motto was Everybody Eats. These niggaz hustled all day every day. Twenty-four hours a day, seven days a week. From sun up to sun down, they were at it, pulling in every dollar that they could. They'd take coins if a crack head had it, they didn't give a fuck. The way they saw it, if it could be spent then it was all good.

The Cream Team was bringing in so much paper that Malik was running out of safes and stashes to put it in. Business was good and everybody was happy. They were hood rich and loving it. The whole crew was iced the fuck out, their pockets were stupid fat, and they were pushing tricked out ass rides. In addition, they had some of the baddest broads sucking and fucking on them. Life wasn't good. It was fucking great.

Gustavo had taken a chance on Malik and it had paid off. The young kingpin was making him a lot of money. When Malik would come to cop, he would bring bags of money so large that it looked like he was going to do his laundry. In time, Gustavo and the Simpsons grew closer. They were business associates as well as good friends. The drug lord took an especially liking to Fear. He was so pleased with the work that he and Wameek had put in on the O'Connor's that he would occasionally call on him to put some other niggaz dicks in the dirt. Fear didn't mind in the least bit, seeing as that he was one of two of Malik's enforcers anyway; the other being Wameek. When mothafuckas got out of line he was already in the middle of knocking their heads off, so he'd just grab a newer gun and put in that work he'd ordered as well. In just three short years, Malik was Top Dawg sitting on the throne of his own empire.

That same day just two hours later

Fear opened the door to Italia's apartment and lumbered his short frame over the threshold. He was exhausted. He wanted to lay it down, but a hot bath was calling his name. He tossed his keys on the coffee table and plopped down on the couch. He removed his jacket and went to pull off his sweatshirt when he heard Italia calling him.

"Babe, is that you?" Italia asked as she came down the staircase.

"Yeah," Fear answered over his shoulder. "Do me a favor and get this fire going for me."

"All right." She headed for the fireplace. When she walked past him he noticed the .45 in her manicured hand. Seeing this brought a smirk to his face. It felt good to have a bitch on his team that could handle herself. Italia was a get money kind of broad with a lady likeness and a gangsta all of her own. Although she and Fear weren't together, she treated him like her man whenever they were together. Granted when they were apart she did her own thing, but he respected it. She had bills to pay like everyone else so she had to hustle niggaz and do other miscellaneous schemes to make a living. With Malik coming off with all of that cocaine from Gustavo, Fear was sure that he was going to be in position to take good care of her. He always wanted to make her his lady but felt that he lacked the proper funding to take care of a chick like her that liked the finer things life had to offer.

Once Italia got the fire going, she turned around to Fear who was in the middle of pulling off his sweatshirt. "Here, let me help you," she said lying the .45 down on the coffee table and assisting him with pulling the sweatshirt over his head. She then removed his Timberlands and helped him out of his Levi's 501 jeans. Next, she pulled off his boxer briefs and grabbed both of his hands, pulling his naked self to his feet. Holding onto his hand, she lead him up the staircase.

"Where are you taking me?" Fear asked.

"Upstairs," Italia answered. "I'm gonna draw you a bath and wash you up."

Fear sat in the tub of hot sudsy water smoking a blunt that Italia had expertly rolled herself. While he indulged in some of the finest exotic weed that had ever been grown, his lady cleaned every inch of his chocolate body with a sponge. He pulled his lips away from the blunt and turned to Italia, grabbing her by the back of the neck, pulling her closer. Their tongues intertwined and they kissed slow and sensually, saliva smacking around inside of their mouths. She then took the blunt from him and partook in it, savoring it before passing it back to him. Ever since before

Fear had claimed Italia as his own, she'd been doing the most for him. She was at his every beckon call and treated him like he was royalty. Not to mention, she never gave him shit about the hours he kept. She knew that he was a street nigga and that the element would take up most of his time. Italia understood what his line of work called for, and all she asked of him was his honesty, love and loyalty. He agreed to set aside a little time for her. So the streets could have him Monday thru Friday, but come the weekend he was all hers. There weren't any ifs, ands, or buts about it.

"Would you die for me, baby?" Fear asked.

"Sho' you right, boo."

"Would you kill for me?"

"Show me that nigga or that bitch and they getting flat-lined."

"Put that on something." He gave her a side eye.

"That's on every thang, baby."

"All right, then." He went back to sucking on the end of his blunt. "I've been thinking."

Yeah."

"It's time we stopped bullshitting and make this thing of ours official."

She smiled and said, "You mean me becoming yo' woman?"

"Fa' sho'." He said like it wasn't a thang.

"I'd love to be." She turned his head to her and they locked lips, passionately and emotionally.

"You know this means you gotta drop all of yo' hoes, right?"

"Notta problem, them niggaz gon'."

He nodded and said, "That's what I wanna hear."

"You won't me to roll out the red carpet for you tonight, babe?" She referred to all of the freaky shit she was down to do that he loved.

"Nah, a nigga beat," Fear lay back in the tub, "You can show ya man what that mouth do, though."

"I got chu faded." Italia dipped her hand into the sudsy water and grabbed Fear's flaccid penis. Gracefully, she worked her hand up and down his grown ass man and watched it grow before her eyes. Once he was good and hard, his dick stood tall and half way out of the water. The head of that mothafucka oozed with pre cum but that didn't stop her from doing what she did next. Without any reserve, she threw her head forth, letting her sopping warm mouth envelope his hardness. The sensation of Italia's mouth caused Fear to moan like a bitch and his toes to curl.

"Ahhhh, Ssssss." He shut his eyes and slipped further down into the water, laying his palm at the top of her head. He rested it there and it shot up and down as her mouth bobbed and slobbered on him. His eyes turned into slits and his mouth hung open. He listened to all of her slurping and sucking for a time. After a while, the blunt that he held pinched between his fingers dropped ashes in the water occasionally, making hissing sounds as the ember hit the wet surface. He relaxed further in his bath and allowed Italia's head game to take him somewhere wet, warm, and pretty. Bahamas here he comes!

CHAPTER TEN
2006

Ponk! Ponk! Ponk!

Wameek bounced the basketball on the court with rhythm. His face was a mask of concentration, sweat dripping from his brows. He clad in a wife beater, jeans and a pair of throwback Jordan's. He had twenty stacks on the line. The money wasn't a thang to him, though. He was more focused on beating his opponent. The idea of losing made him sick to his fucking stomach. He hated it with a passion which was why he couldn't lose. Off to the side stood Fear, bare chest and sweaty in a pair of black Dickie shorts. His hands were resting on his hips and he was watching his older cousin closely. Malik stood beside him on his Kawasaki Ninja, the money of the bet nestled inside of his helmet as he watched on, anxious to see how all of this was going to play out.

Wameek lifted the Spalding and let it fly. The basketball bounced off one side of the rim to the other and fell into the net less basket. "Uhh!" He swung on the arm, gritting after making the shot. "That's what I'm talkin' about, baby, gimmie my mothafuckin' money." He approached his brother, flexing his fingers for him to give him his winnings. Fear stood there wearing a crooked grin as he watched his cousin collect his winnings from his sibling's helmet. He came out of the helmet with two handfuls of dead white men, kissing them hard and smiling. "Payday, homeboy." He went right along counting up the money with his cousin and brother watching. "You win some and you lose some. It's all a part of the game, baby boy." He went to pat Fear on his cheek and he smacked his hand away. The impact of flesh against flesh made a smacking sound.

"Don't put cho hands on me, dawg! You ain't the boss of this family and I for damn sure notta young boy looking to make my bones." He frowned, not feeling his kin trying to play him out like he wasn't built. "I've been done jumped off the porch. Now you tryna run that shit back or what?" He went on to count up the dead presidents in his hand, licking his thumb before accounting for each and every bill.

Malik's head swung from left to right looking at the exchange between his loved ones.

"Nigga, you ain't said shit, run that fifty back."

"Nah, double or nothing."

Wameek frowned, looking like he wasn't trying to fuck with all of that action.

"What chu scared, sweetheart? Pull ya thong out cha ass, Shameeka, and let's run this shit back." He dangled the keys to his Mercedes Benz CLK. It was blacked out with black rims and a chrome lip. That bitch looked like it belonged in some rapper nigga'z music video.

"You talkin' pink slips now?" Wameek asked fearfully. He loved money but he loved his Hummer even more. That thang was milk white with all black interior, looking like a straight up Oreo cookie.

"Yes, nigga, pink slips. If you scared then go to church," Fear taunted him. "I gotta 'nough loot to pay the difference on that big ass tank you rolling."

"Whewwww!" Malik busted up laughing with a leather glove fist to his mouth, instigating shit. "Baby bruh, I know you not gon' let the young reli talk to you like that, are you? I know you not about to let that ride, show 'em up, Meek."

Wameek grew angry and arched his eyebrows. He clenched his jaws so tightly that they throbbed.

"Bet mothafucka!" He dropped the money and his car keys into motorcycle helmet. His cousin was right behind him tossing his stake on the bet and his car's keys. "You ain't said notta damn thang, ol' young ass nigga. You forgot that chu ain't the only nigga out here gettin' money? Tuh, we can do this shit all day. I gotta 'nough dough to keep shooting this ball until your arms fall off. I tried to warn your lil' ass about fuckin' with me on this diamond, I does this, before the street dreams I was the Michael Jordan of South Central. You betta ask somebody." Wameek locked into a tense stare with Fear, dribbling the basketball between his legs with expertise. His legs shifted back and forth rapidly, keeping up the fast space. He cracked a devilish smile, feeling that he had one up on his little cousin.

Back in the day, Wameek was nice on the court. He was predicted to be the next best thing to hit the NBA since Kobe Bryant. His face was on the cover of every sports magazine you could name and he'd been the talk of the world. It was safe to say that he had the world at his feet, but he threw it all away to run the streets. To him being a superstar basketball player was cool, but being a gangsta was even better. The hood whispered with talks of him being a goddamn fool for letting the opportunity slip through his fingers, but he didn't care he was living out his fantasy. And no matter how dumb of a fantasy it may have seemed to everyone else, it was his to live. "I'm not gon' stop 'til you leave out this mothafucka wearing nothing but your socks and draws." He stopped flexing and bounced the basketball at a steady pace.

"Ain't nobody tryna hear yo' failed attempts at basketball stardom, nigga." Fear waved him off with a twisted face. "Shoot that mothafucking ball, Blood."

"Oh, I'ma shoot it, you ain't even gotta worry about that, homeboy." He looked to Malik as he continued to bounce the ball, nodding to the motorcycle helmet in his possession which contained the money. "You make sure no one runs off with that helmet."

"Anybody tries to run off with this helmet gon' die from a heat stroke," Malik's face contracted with hostility as he tapped the bulge on his waistline. He stayed strapped at all times. A nigga trying to steal that money from him was gone end up becoming a casualty of a botched robbery.

"Alright then, same game, my nigga, best three out of five shots. A hunnit grand, winner takes all?" He looked at Fear.

"Yeah, that's right." He nodded his agreement and smirked, folding his arms across his chest.

Wameek faced the basket. Bouncing the Spalding, sweat trickling from his forehead, he stole a glance at Fear. He was smirking with his arms folded across his chest.

I'ma wipe that smug look right off yo' fuckin' face, lil' punk ass nigga tryna show me up out here. Nigga don't know I'm not one to fuck with on this court, on my sista rest in peace, Wameek's heart raged inside of his chest. Although he was just popping that shit the pressure he felt on his shoulders was immense. He wished he hadn't opened his big fucking mouth and had walked off with that paper. It was too late now. His mouth had written a check that his ass hoped that it could cash.

Wameek was passing through the hood stunting in his brand new H2 Hummer chopping it up with the people and spreading dollars around to the little ghetto kids, when he saw Fear out on the court at Trinity Park shooting one of their workers lights out for fun. Not wanting to miss his chance to upstage his little cousin, he took off all of his jewelry and stripped down to his wife beater. He had it on his mind to challenge his kin to a shootout, fifty racks a game. Now here he was with a hundred grand on the line as well as his pride.

Wameek raised the ball and released it from his dry ashy palms. The basketball hit the backboard and fell into the basket. Fear applauded him and kicked the ball back out to him. Wameek wiped his sweaty forehead with his hand, bounced the ball twice, blew hard and sunk the Spalding into the basket. He put the ball up three more times; making the next two but missing the last one. He smiled devilishly again as he handed the ball off to Fear and stepped behind the backboard. He thought the best he could do was tie the game or fall short a basket, but there was no way he'd make all five shots.

Wameek laughed and rubbed his hands together greedily as his relative bounced the ball, about to take his first shot. Swoosh! Swoosh! Swoosh! With each shot came the change of Wameek's facial expression. He was heated now. His face contorted with anger and his arms had folded across his chest. By the time Fear had made his forth basket, his body was warm all over. He was about ready to give his kin them hands. His eyes held a glimmer of hope when Fear shot the ball for the fifth time. The Spalding circled the rim slowly causing the younger twin's heart to beat crazily inside of his chest. His hope was soon shattered into a million pieces when the ball fell into the basket. He shut his eyes and silently said fuck.

"That's game, Bleed." Fear smirked, feeling himself after the victory. He moved to collect his winnings and frowned when he saw Wameek snatching the helmet away from his brother and grabbed all of the money from out of it, dropping a set of the keys to the ground while doing so. He turned around to Fear unbuckling his belt and unzipping his jeans. Bending over, he stuck the money inside of his boxer briefs and brushed it back and forth across his sweaty asshole and nut sack. Fear glared at him and clenched his fists tightly. It was possible to cook steak on his head he was so hot then. Malik shut his eyes and massaged the bride of his nose seeing what his brother was doing. Smiling fiendishly, Wameek slowly pulled the money out and held it up. He then brought it to his nose and shut his eyes as he inhaled his funk from the bills, a smile spread across his face.

"Ahhhhhhh!" he looked to Fear, still smiling. "Now that's some nice stank on it."

"Motha…" Fear took off after Wameek, ready to lock ass with him.

"Oh shit!" Malik kicked his kickstand down with the heel of his sneaker, relieving his motorcycle. He snatched off his leather gloves and stuffed them inside of his back pocket as he ran to grab his cousin before he could reach his sibling. He'd just snatched him up, when his brother dropped his money and squared up to get busy.

"That's it, that's fucking it!" Fear swung and kicked, trying to get loose from his cousin's iron hold. "Lemmie go, Lik, I'ma beat that ass real good!"

"Calm down, man." He backed him over to the gate, leaving his evil eyes staring over his shoulder at his brother. Fear was clenching his teeth so hard that he thought that they were going to break. "We don't need to be fighting each other, fam. The enemy is out there." He glanced over his shoulder and pointed out into the street, cars racing back and forth in it. "The eses, the crips, the Feds, other black people, shiddd, y'all niggaz betta wake up 'cause we're all we got." He looked back and forth between his brother and his cousin. They were still locked into a stare mad dogging one another, chest jumping up and down, fists clenching. "Y'all hear me?" he looked between them again, waiting for their answers but they didn't say nothing. "I said, do y'all two mothafuckaz hear me?" he spoke with a low growl. Wameek and Fear's mad dogging ceased shortly after and they unclenched their fists, causing the veins to vanish from their temples. They took deep breaths and their hatred for one another smoothed over for the time being. "Alright then, y'all hug that shit out, we fam up out this bitch." He waved his hands signaling for them to embrace. Reluctantly they approached and hugged, both of them rolling their eyes like it was killing them to do so.

"Get cho money, AJ." Malik pointed to the ground where the degraded money was.

"Nah, man, I don't want that shit no more." Fear frowned, waving his hand at the thought of picking up the cash he'd won fair and square.

"Get the money and give it to 'em, bro." Malik ordered his twin.

"I ain't 'bout to pick up shit. That's his loot." He balled up his face and folded his arms across his chest, like to say *And that's final.*

Malik blew hot air and shook his head like it was a goddamn shame how they were acting. Hearing whistling,he looked up and saw crack head Tyrone walking happily up the sidewalk like he didn't have a care in the world. "Yo' Tyrone!" he called out, stealing the fiend's attention. He looked over at him with raised eyebrows. When the man' s face registered in his mental he smiled because he knew that any time that he called on him that he was about to make some money to buy some crack with.

"What chu need, Big Time?" Tyrone asked in an at your service kind of voice, fingers grasping the holes in the gate.

"You wanna make some money?" He inquired.

"Helllll yeah, I wanna make some money," he replied like *Nigga, you don't even have to ask that.*

"Get this money up for me, Big Dawg." He pointed down to the money.

"Alright." He climbed over the gate and jumped down, landing hunched over but then standing up. While he was gathering the loose bills, Wameek and Fear were projecting hateful eyes at one another, mouthing threats. "Say, uh, what chu want me to do with this?" He held up his filthy, tattered T-shirt which he'd used to pile the money in and tie it up.

"Toss it inside the trunk of my new ride." Fear smiled triumphantly, jiggling the keys to Wameek's Hummer taunting. His eyes shot over to him to see if his rubbing his victory in his face was affecting him and it surely was because that nigga was pissed off. Fear tossed the keys to Tyrone and he grabbed them out of the air. "You got L's?"

"My driver's license has been expired "85," he answered.

"Don't matter, long as you can drive," Fear told him. "I want chu to drive my new toy out to my spot."

"Okay. I can do that," he said joyfully.

"Cool. You do that and half that trap is yours."

"My man, that's a sure bet." Tyrone smiled and ran off to the Hummer. Hearing Fear calling him back, he stopped and turned around.

With a serious look in his eyes he said to him, "If you try some slick shit, you won't make it off this block. Keep it one hunnit, family."

"Oh, I will, Big Time, you ain't gotta worry about me."

"Sho' you right." He nodded and the crack head proceeded.

"Lucky mothafucka," Wameek said under his breath.

"Luck didn't have nothing to do with it; I'm nice with mine, homie." Fear caught what he said.

"Damn, who that?" Malik threw his head back at a sexy, young thang moving down the sidewalk like she was on the runway at a fashion show. She slim and curvaceous with an ass shaped like teardrop. She was wearing black sunglasses; a black wife beater and Daisy Dukes that put hear chunky ass cheeks out on display.

Fear was smiling like Cheshire cat when he saw the vision of perfection. But that expression vanished from his face when he realized who the eye candy actually was.

"That's jail bait." He said to no one in particular, eyes lingering on her.

"What chu mean?" Malik looked to him with lines across his forehead.

"That's Mitch Dollas lil' cousin, Tamara," he informed him, "Lil' momma hotta than an African summa."

"Oh," The excitement drained from Malik's face. He loved beautiful grown women, not little ass girls.

"Man, I ain't even tryna hear all of that none sense." Wameek waved them both off, continuing his ogling of the young lady. "Yo' what's brackin', lil' momma?" He hollered out, throwing up both of his arms like a field goal was good.

The dark skinned cutie lifted her black sunglasses and eyed him seductively as she sucked on a cherry Tootsie Roll pop. She flashed her perfect smile and licked her top lip, showcasing the bulb of her pearl tongue ring. With that, she approached the gate, her ample ass jiggling like a bowl of Jell-O as she walked along like a horse. Malik and Fear exchanged confused expression seeing Wameek jogging over to the gate to spit some G at the underage girl. They watched as he chopped it up with the statutory rape charge, programming her number into his cell phone.

"My nigga she's only thirteen years old," Fear told Malik.

"Get the fuck outta here." He looked at him with his eyes wide and his mouth hanging open. "That lil' broad built like she twenty five."

"I know." Fear shook his head like it was a goddamn shame. "Her fast ass 'bout to get hella niggaz killed behind her." He looked on as Wameeka and Tamara continued to chop it up.

"Either that are sent away on an iron vacation behind that underage pussy." He watched his brother closely as well. "No, thank you, I'll pass 'cause I ain't beat."

Just then Wameek came jogging back to them smiling from ear to ear. He stopped before his loved ones seeing the perturbed expression son their faces caused him to frown.

"'Sup?"

"Lil' momma is only thirteen."

"So, and?" He shrugged like it wasn't a big deal.

"Mannn," Wameek smacked his lips. "I ain't tryna hear none of that. Bitch think she's grown I'ma show her what grown folks do, ya Griff me?"

"You're a real fucking scum bag, you know that?" Fear looked at him disgustingly. That vile ass nigga made his stomach twist in knots.

Wameek spit on the curb and said, "Whatever nigga. I tell you this though, before it's all said and done...I'ma be all up in them guts, believe that."

Fear sighed and shook his head saying, "Alright, I'm up." He dapped up his people and jogged across the street to his whip, fired that thang up and peeled off. Crack head Tyrone was pulling off right behind him.

**

The sun had begun to set on The City of Angels causing the sky to turn a murky blue. A Mercedes Benz was burning up the streets fast.

Vrooooooom!

The vehicle shot through a light just as it turned red, causing debris to fly and papers to float. Tyrone was a light behind, driving at the speed limit so he wouldn't get pulled over. The last thing he wanted to do was to get pulled over and jeopardize getting his cut of the winnings. As soon as Fear flew past another light that had just turned red, the headlights of a black "06 Chevy Impala came on. It drove out of the 7/11 parking lot and turned on its red and blue flashing lights, its engine roaring as it went into pursuit of the Charger.

Blurp! Blurp!

The very familiar sound of the chirping police siren stole Fear's attention. He looked up into the rearview mirror and saw the red and blue flashing light on top of the Chevy Impala. He rolled his eyes and looked off to the side mumbling under his breath. He was so not in the mood to deal with the law, especially after having dealt with Wameek and his bullshit earlier that day.

Fear pulled over to the side of the street under the dim illumination of a street light post. This was the perfect spot for the law officer to engage him. Because he'd be less likely to try some corrupted type of shit like beat his ass to a bloody pulp or plant some dope on him. Fear slouched down in the driver seat and eyeballed the side view mirror. He watched as an African American detective stepped out of the Chevy Impala, one Timberland boot at a time. He rocked a crisp white T-shirt underneath a black leather motorcycle jacket. A gold necklace laced with a gold cross flooded with diamonds hung loosely around his neck. The cross rose and fell against his chest as he walked forth. A gold shield was attached to his black leather belt. Fear caught gleaming glimpses of it as he strode in his direction. Through the reflection of the side view mirror's glass, he saw the man's face. The nigga looked familiar, but he couldn't quite place his face.

"Well, well, well, if it isn't my old buddy Fear," Broli leaned down into the driver side window and locked eyes with Fear, a sinister smile forming on his lips. Lyle Broli was a tall, muscular built dude of an almond hue. He had black rings around his eyes and matching lips having been a pot head for majority of his life. When it came to cops he was one of the craftiest to have ever worn a shield. He was about a dollar and he wasn't above breaking the law to get it. This was the cop that had pulled Fear and Wameek over the day they had procured the thirty kilos from Gustavo three years ago. Back then he was just a fairly new uniform, but now he was a hardened law enforcer that had made his bones.

"What's up, Broli?" Fear rolled his eyes and blew his hot breath.

"Ain't shit," Broli claimed, eyes scanning the backseat as he chewed on gum. "How 'bout you?"

"I'm good, family." He nodded to the soft music flowing from the speakers and tapped his fingers in a rhythm on the steering wheel, acting as if he didn't have a care in the world. That wasn't the farthest from the truth though because he had that thang stashed between the seat and the console.

The crooked badge nodded his head and took a step back; eyeballing the Benz like it was a thick broad with a fat ass. He whistled, impressed with the eye candy before his brown eyes.

"Yeah, I can see that," Broli said, appreciating the luxurious vehicle. "How much this pretty lil' thang run you, Big Dawg?"

"Ah, man," Fear waved his hand. "This old thang ain't nothing. I brought this from one of those car auctions a couple of years ago." He downplayed the sixty thousand dollar car.

"Man, I can't hear a goddamn thang with that bullshit chu playin'. Turn that shit down," he spoke aggravated. Fear complied with his order and he rested his arm on the windowsill of the Benz. "Now what were you sayin'?"

"I said, I got this old thang from an auction a couple of years ago."

"Yeah, I just bet." He gave him the side eye and twisted his lips like You must think I'm a fucking fool. "I'll tell you, I'm in the wrong business 'cause from the look of things, that drug money has gotta be real sweet."

"Drug money?" He raised an eyebrow like that shit was so absurd. "Man, I told you my daddy die and left me…"

"Save it, nigga. You and those cousins of yours are some real flamboyant type of mothafuckaz. Y'all like fancy cars and flashy things."

"If you say so."

"Nah, bitch, I know so." He caught an attitude, mad dogging him.

It was all true. Malik was one of the city's biggest drug dealers and he and Wameek were his enforcers. The three of them was young and getting it. They copped whatever they wanted, it didn't matter to them what was on the price tag. If they wanted it they got it, it was just as simple as that. Broli had hit the nail on the head but Fear wasn't about to admit that he was right though. Besides, it wasn't what he knew it was what he could prove. He knew that if he could prove a mothafucking thing than his black ass would be en route to the precinct in handcuffs right that minute.

"I gotta say the three Musketeers have blown up. The day I stopped you and the whack job cousin of yours, Wameek, I knew you two niggaz were up to something," Broli confessed. "I could smell the dope in the trunk of that Mustang latched to the back of that tow truck." Fear frowned and his stomach twisted hearing him reveal this. He'd always felt that the law dog had suspected something back then but he thought nothing of it because he'd let them go that day. "I kept an eye on y'all from a far and watched the power moves y'all made. I smiled like a proud father when I realized that I was as right as rain. I decided to fallback and allow y'all to do y'all thang and become these larger than life figures so that I could bust yo' mothafuckin' asses." He relayed angrily. "Things have changed now though. I'm willin' to make a compromise. You and yo' relatives can push all of the poison you want just as long as y'all kick up those taxes to me." Fear glanced through the rearview mirror and saw Tyrone driving up in the Hummer he'd won from Wameek. "Now I've already relayed the message to big cuz, you know, Malik? Said he'll think it over but he hasn't got back yet. You tell that dick sucka he's got three days to come up off that paper or my people gon' find 'em floatin' face down in a river, you got that?"

"Loud and clear," Fear answered, looking up in the rearview mirror again. His attitude was very nonchalant then, like he could care less about what he was talking about.

"Good." Broli wrote something down and handed it to him. Fear looked it over frowning. "A broken tail light?" he hollered out, watching Broli's scandalous ass walk back to his vehicle through the side view mirror.

"Yeah, taillight." He stopped at the rear of the Benz, kicking the light until it exploded into broken shards.

"Shieettt!" Fear slammed his fist down onto the steering wheel.

The crooked badge continued on to his Impala whistling Dixie. Jumping behind the wheel, he cranked up its engine and drove back in the direction that the Hummer was coming from. Tyrone drove to a stop behind Fear's Benz where he stayed until he eventually drove off and he was able to follow him.

CHAPTER ELEVEN
2006

Club Code Blue was where it was that night so you know The Simpsons and their clique had to fall through in that bitch deep as a mothafucka. Fear, Malik and their crew were kicking it inside of the V.I.P section. The air was so heavy with weed smoke that it was easy to catch a contact. Thanks to Malik who kept at least three blunts in rotation amongst them. There were six empty gold bottles of Ace of Spades on their table and one unopened one. Every time a bottle would get half way empty Malik would order up another one. He tipped the waitress a Benjamin for every bottle she brought back to the table. He wanted the whole spot to know that his crew was in the house and they were doing big things and making major moves.

"Aye, this mothafucka live tonight," Malik hollered to Fear over the blaring music, having just finished dancing with some cutie with a great big booty to R. Kelly's Go Getta. He kept a bottle Ace of Spades in one hand, while the other groped her thick thighs and bodacious. He sat the bottle down on the table and used a couple of napkins to pat the beads of sweat from his forehead.

"Hell yeah, man," Fear replied. He'd just finished dancing with a sexy young thang and was now pouring up a champagne flute. He watched the chick he'd been dancing with across his line of vision with her girlfriends in tow. She smiled and blew him a kiss from her palm. Once she was swallowed up by the crowd, he pulled out his cellular and searched his contacts for her number. As soon as he came across the name Kathy he deleted it. He would not dare step out on Italia. She meant too much to him over a cheap thrill. That was his soul mate so she had his heart.

"Say, handsome, I'ma go powder my nose, I'll be right back." She eyed him lustfully as she traced his face with a French tipped nail. This was the same woman he'd been dancing with.

"Alright." He looked at her like she was an ice cold glass of water and he was thirsty, watching that enormous ass of hers dance as she headed off to get fresh.

"Yo' you seen Wameek?" Malik inquired about the whereabouts of his younger brother.

"Yeah, he was kicking it to some broad earlier," He relayed, scanning the establishment for his cousin.

"There he is?" Malik nodded to the dance floor.

"Where?" Fear asked with narrowed eyelids, looking about for their loved one.

Malik threw his arm around his neck and pulled him closer. His mouth was near his ear as he spoke and pointed out his brother. "That's him right there, gettin' it in with that lil' ho right there, see?" he looked from his Fear to out where he'd spotted his sibling. Wameek grinding up against the ass of some hood rat with his hands crossed and planted on her back. She was wobbling those loose, juicy cheeks against the growing bulge in his jeans. Her black dress was above her waistline and her sky blue thong was visible for all to see. She was looking at him from over her shoulder with a seductive smile, her tongue tracing her top lip. Her long cornrows were frizzy from the heat of the congested space. And her face, chest and shoulders were glistening from her perspiration. Fear narrowed his eyelids trying to remember where he'd seen the girl before. Although he couldn't I.D her she looked familiar as hell. It was until Wameek pulled her head back by the ends of her cornrows, bit down on his inner jaw and started dry humping her from behind that he recognized her.

"Oh shit!" Fear's eyes bulged.

"What? What's up?" Malik questioned with great concerned.

"Man, that's Mitch's people that he's basically fucking out there!" he angrily pointed at the chick Wameek was grinding up on.

"Wait, you mean, Tamara, that lil' broad that was walkin' by the park earlier today," he frowned, looking at him like say it ain't so.

"Yep." Fear nodded, eyes focused on Wameek and the girl.

"How the fuck did her young ass get up in here?" he wondered.

"Man, I don't know but he's looking to go out bad behind some underage pussy." He shook his head like, I can't believe this stupid ass nigga.

"Let me stop this shit 'fore this nigga end up witta charge." Malik moved to head in his twin's direction and bumped into someone holding a champagne flute, spilling on his brown suede blazer. "Damn." He looked down at the darkened spots of his blazer he'd gotten from the collision. When he looked back up homeboy carrying the flute was fuming mad. It appeared that steam was rising from his head and his eyes were laser red.

"Sorry about that, homie, let me give you a lil' somethin' to take yo' shit to the cleaners." He pulled out his money which was secured by a money-clip. After pulling it off, he licked his thumb and counted off a few bills.

"Yeah, break mine off!" He popped shit, looking down at all of the dead men in his hand.

"Another asshole." Malik shook his head, not pressed for the bullshit. He was having a good night and wasn't about to let this nigga fuck it up. He came up with two one hundred dollar bills and tried to pass it to the man. The nigga he'd collided with looked at it like he'd just wiped his ass with it.

"Oh, nigga you gon' have to come up with a lil' mo' then that, that's for damn sure." He looked at him like he was bat sit crazy for trying to give him two hundred dollars to get his shirt dry cleaned.

"My nigga, fuck is yo'…" Fear was cut short by a hand to his chest by Malik which calmed him down.

"I got this." Malik told him. By this time all of his crew slowly began to assemble around him, feeling their leader's life being in danger.

"Fuck you think, you scaring something 'cause you brought a couple niggaz here witchu? Squuaad up!" the man hollered but kept his threatening eyes on Malik. Instantly his niggaz appeared out of nowhere, gathering around him. The club was jumping so with the music and a good time in the atmosphere no one was paying any attention to the shit that was about to hit the fan.

"I see you got cho goons on deck, true that." Malik nodded, holding his wrists at his waist. "But understand somethin', Blood. Although we're few we're crazy." With that said, he snatched a gold bottle from off the tray of a barmaid passing by. Lunging forward, he gritted and slammed the bottle of his head causing it to explode. Broken glass and alcohol suds coated the victim's head and he staggered backwards, falling on his back. That right there set off The Ghetto Royal Rumble. Fear came out of nowhere slinging his chair and bursting it against the opposition's torso. The club broke out in chaos niggaz and bitches were flying each and every way trying to get the fuck out of there. Punches, kicks, tackles, and bites occurred. Not long after the lights came on, niggaz were still throwing them hands.

Eventually the police turned up and shut that shit down. They hauled some of the brawlers off to jail, harassed others and let some go. Once Fear was let out the backseat of a police cruiser after having his name ran through the database, he searched the crowd for Malik. His heart raged a war inside of his chest when he didn't see his people amongst the rest of the patrons. He thought for sure that The Man had whisked him away. Finally, he spotted the oldest twin in the backseat of another police cruiser.

The only thing Malik had on his record was a gun charge from three years ago. He did straight time so he wasn't on parole, but he knew that The Boys were gone put some bullshit up in the mix. His name was as hot as fish grease in the hood since he had been supplying the majority of the hustlers from around his way. The young kingpin was prepared for whatever One Time came at him with and he was positive that it would be something. See, he'd already overheard a couple of them talking about riding him around the city and questioning him until he finally given them something on himself or someone he was affiliated with. This was a scare tactic that the police often used to try to gather intelligence on the happenings in the streets and sometimes it even worked. But niggaz like Malik were cut from a different cloth. His G didn't bend nor fold for nobody. That's just how he was built.

"I'll be alright, just go." Malik mouthed to Fear and threw his head in the direction of his vehicle. "I'll be straight."

Fear pounded the Blood gang sign to his chest and his cousin gave him a nod. With that, he took off running in the opposite direction. Right before the big brawl went down, Fear saw Wameek dipping off with Tamara. He could tell by the look in her youthful eyes that she was good and tipsy and a prime candidate to get fucked that night. It had been an hour since then so he was positive that Wameek had went up in her, and knowing his dog ass, he more than likely didn't bother to strap up. Fear hopped behind the wheel of his ride and fired it up. It slightly vibrated and the blaring music within its confines caused it to rattle, its side view mirrors shaking. He threw the car in drive and pulled off hoping his cousin hadn't made the mistake of sleeping with an underage girl. Although he had a feeling that he had, he would pray that he didn't.

"Please, God, don't let it go down like that." He shut his eyes for a moment's prayer. After peeling his eyelids open, he gripped the steering wheel firmly and mashed the gas pedal.

Vrooooom!

He blew through a street light just as it turned red, fingers crossed that he wasn't too late.

Forty five minutes later

Fear knocked on the front door of Wameek's home for about five minutes before deciding to walk around to the side of the house to see if he could see anyone through the bedroom window. He trekked along the side of the house until he met the last bedroom window. He placed his face against the glass with his hands cupped around his temples. The bedroom was pitch black so he couldn't see a thing. Hearing faint noises, he pressed his ear up against the glass and heard faint grunting and muffled screaming, three folds formed across his forehead and his nose crinkled. He knocked on the window but the grunting continued so he knocked harder this time.

"Who is it?" Wameek snapped, heatedly.

"Fear, nigga, open up."

"Gimmie a minute."

"Alright," Fear replied before heading back to the front of the house to the door. He occasionally looked over his shoulders as he waited for the front door to be unlocked. Finally, he heard someone shuffling around inside before the locks of the door was being undid. Before he knew it the door was being pulled open and Wameek was standing in front of him. His hair was matted over his face and he was breathing like a raging bull. His hairy chest heaved up and down as he held the door open, form glistening wet with beads of sweat. His jeans were unbuckle and half way off of his waistline, showcasing his nappy public hairs. He stood aside as his little cousin brushed passed him. After locking the front door, he turned around and that's when he spotted the scratches sprawled down his neck.

"Fuck you wanted?" He asked, lighting up a cigarette and sitting down on the couch.

"What happened to ya neck?" Fear's brows furrowed, staring at his wounds.

"What?" Wameek frowned, touching his neck and coming away with bloody fingertips. "Oh this ain't 'bout nothing, got into a lil' something something earlier. Baby girl was a straight up freak. I'm talking nympho, reli." He capped with a smile, gold grill sparkling like it had been polished to a finish.

"Right." Fear nodded, looking at him accusingly.

His eyes wandered over to the bedroom door. It was cracked open. He felt an icy finger travel up his spine causing him to shiver. Something was wrong and he could feel it. Fear looked from the door to his twin cousin. Wameek wore a dumb founded expression on his face as he took tokes from the Joe, allowing smoke to exhaust from his nose and mouth. His eyes looked up from the floor and settled on his little cousin's.

Wameek shrugged and said, "East the deal?"

Fear narrowed his eyelids at him before starting off towards the bedroom. The youngest of the twins continued to sit on the couch mouthing Shit as he watched his kin head for the door. All he could do was wait for his reaction once he'd found what was inside of his bedroom.

Fear slowly pushed the bedroom door open, cutting a shining light inside. He sniffed the air, smelling a repugnant odor lingering. The stench was strong. It was one of shit and piss mixed with death. It made him gag a little but he held onto his lunch. He flipped the light-switch on and the illumination gave life to a horrifying sight. Tamara, the young girl that Wameek lusted after that day at the park, was lying on her stomach on the bed. Her pussy was swollen and her asshole was blown out, looking like bloody hamburger meat. She had welts that lead up her back and ended at her shoulders. Fear's forehead crinkled as he rounded the bed to get a good look at her, face frowned up. A telephone cord was wrapped around her neck so tightly that it left a red ring. She'd been strangled to death. Her eyes were staring up at the ceiling at nothing and her mouth was stretched open. He moved in and placed two fingers to her neck to check her pulse. Discovering that she was dead, he closed his eyes and said a prayer that his parents had taught him before crossing his heart in the sign of the crucifix.

Fear unraveled the cord from around the young girl's neck and pushed her over on her back. He shook his head hating to have to see someone so young have their life cut short like an umbilical cord after birth. With a brush of his palm, he closed her eyes and covered her up with a blanket.

"I'm sorry," he said regretfully, his tone loud enough for her to hear if she'd been alive. After kissing his fingers, he touched them to the area of the fabric where her forehead was. Rising to his feet and turning around, he found Wameek standing in the doorway taking casual draws from his Joe, looking at the blanketed dead body of the poor girl as if it wasn't a big deal. The sick bastard's eyes wandered up from the blanket and settled on his cousin. He could see him clenching and unclenching his jaws and clutching his fists so tight that his knuckles threatened to burst through the skin. The young nigga was hot, the burner of the stove hot. His eyes looked like two glowing embers only underlined this.

Wameek shrugged, blowing smoke from out of his nose and mouth. "Fuck you gon' do about it?

"Monsterrrr!" Fear's eyes widen to their capacity and he shrilled aloud, head quaking like it was about to explode from off of his shoulders. He took off in his cousin's direction moving like a track star after hearing a starter pistol being fired at a race. Wameek let the square drop from his lips and reached for his waistline. Once he grabbed air, he looked to where he had his gun stashed and found that it wasn't there. His head snapped up looking to the dresser, his banger was there beside the ashtray and lamp. Fuck! He thought right before his relative's fist went crashing into his mouth. Bwap! White exploded before his eyes and his buff ass went slamming up against the wall inside of the hallway. He went to slide down to the carpet but the little nigga was like a vicious ass pit bull, on his mothafucking ass. Bwap! Crack! Bwhack! Boop! Bwock! He went to work on his torso and head, whipping it like a speed bag in a boxing gym. The look on the maniac's face was of hurt and confusion. He didn't know if he was being hit with fists or sledge hammers.

Fear grabbed him by the back of the neck and threw him up against the wall; he bumped his head and winced. Shots to the kidneys made him buckle but he swung his arm backwards in a futile attempt because the shorter man was able to duck it. When he came back up, two haymakers sent him staggering back and crashing to the floor. Grimacing, he struggled to lift his head and when he finally did he saw his attacker approaching with ease, as if he just knew that he wasn't going anywhere until he was done with him. Seeing a dark silhouette en route in his direction with clenched fists at its sides scared the shit out of him. Terrified, he got upon his hands and knees crawling away as fast as he could. He'd just crossed the threshold into the living room when he heard a familiar sound. Click! Clack! He and that sound were well acquainted. His gun made this noise on several occasions and it was always before he rocked a nigga to sleep. Now it was his turn to be on the receiving end of a bullet and he couldn't help growing queasy and feeling his bowels shift. At the moment he believed he was feeling what an animal felt like before being hunted.

"I finally understand this shit now, Wa," Fear spoke in a calm and steady voice. "Our operation is the body and you're the infected arm. You have to be severed before the disease is able to spread…" he kicked him in the ass and he fell forward, his face mashing hard into the carpet. He stomped his back and kicked him in the side causing him to howl in pain. "Turn over, you fucking miscreant." Wameek slowly turned over on his back holding his side, his face a mask of excruciation. Fear pinned his arms to the carpet by placing his knees against them, he grabbed him by the lower half of his face hard, making his lips perk up. "Open yo' mouth, nigga." He gritted.

"Fuck you!" Wameek spat muffled.

Whack! Crack! Thwap!

A couple of whacks upside his head caused him to holler and then that thang was shoved into the back of his throat. He gagged feeling that hard metal filling his mouth.

"Gaaghhhh!" His eyes bulged and tears ran around his face rapidly. He squeezed his eyelids shut and waited for the blast that would leave him on the swings on The Devil's playground.

Fear turned his head as he held a hand behind the back of his weapon to protect his face from the blood and brain splatter. His face twisted and he made to pull the trigger when he heard a voice at the front door. He looked up and saw Malik gripping his banger with both hands, the lethal end trained on him.

"Get offa 'em, Blood," Malik spoke with seriousness in his eyes, finger settled on the trigger.

"This nigga is an abomination and he has to be stopped!" Fear looked up at him then down at his brother, trying to see should he sacrifice himself in order to rid the world of the monster.

"I know, bro." Hotness stung Malik's eyes and tears came flooding down his face. He hated to be in a position where he'd have to pop one in his cousin, but his hands were tied. If he didn't do something he was for sure that his relative would go through with murking out his sibling. That was something that he couldn't have. His brother was his heart, it didn't matter what he'd done or what he'd do in the future. That fact would always stand. "But that's my baby brother, and we came into this world together, ya Griff me?" He took his hand away from his gun and wiped the fleeing tears from his face, sniffling.

"Have you even seen what this filth has done to this fourteen year old girl in there, huh?" Fear belted out as he glanced at the bedroom door and threw a hand at it. Tears outlined the rims of his eyes and made to spill, but he blinked them back, eyelashes batting them. "He...he...he...fuck this!" He went to blow Wameek's brains out, but the shouting stopped him.

"Don't!" Malik shouted, spit flying from his lips. "Don't chu do that, man! Don't chu fuckin' do it! Don't put me in this position where I have to kill you! I love you, man! I don't need this shit on my conscience!" He locked eyes with his little cousin, tension and intensity passing through them both. The next move could be fatal for either of them. It was all left in their hands. They watched one another's eyes and the slow rising and falling of each other's chests. Both wanted to test each other's gangsta, but that would be foolish. They already knew how this would end if they followed through with their threats because they had knowledge of one another's pedigree.

Malik's eyes darted to his cousin's finger behind the trigger guard; he saw his finger curling tighter around the trigger about to squeeze it.

"Please." He looked to him with pleading eyes, hoping that he'd change his mind. God, don't make me have to pop my lil' relative's helmet, I love this nigga to death but I love my bro more.

Fear blew hot air from his nose and mouth, shaking his head as he whispered something under his breath. He looked down at Wameek who was staring back up at him, eyes waiting to see what his next move was going to be. The maniac breathed easily when the cold steel was taken out of his grill. Fear stuck out his hand and he looked at it like it was rigged to explode before eventually taking it. He pulled his relative up to his feet, wearing a solemn expression as he stared into his eyes.

Malik sighed and wiped the beads of sweat from his forehead with the back of his hand, tucking his head bussa on his waistline.

"You, all right?" He addressed his younger brother feeling on his head, chest and arms, like he was a kid that had hurt himself falling off of his bicycle.

"I'm good." His brother responded, hateful eyes trained on their younger cousin.

"Let me see what the sitch' is back here." He journeyed down the hallway, emerging into the bedroom and flipping on the light-switch.

Fear and Wameek stood in the hallway mad dogging each other, the corner of their top lips twitching. They looked like a couple of angry wolves.

"Oh my God!" Malik staggered out into the corridor with his fist to his mouth, like he was trying not to vomit.

His eyes crept up from the floor and landed on his brother's, eyebrows arching and nose scrunching. He stormed down the hallway toward his sibling, speed walking.

"Bro, what's up? Why you trippin'?" Wameek frowned and lifted his hands in surrender.

"You piece of shit!" He slapped him across the face viciously, causing him to fall back against the wall inside of the corridor. He put up his hands, but he stayed on him, slapping him violently. Specks of blood flew everywhere and he slid down to the carpet, holding up a leg to shield himself. His big brother kneeled down to him continuing his assault.

Slap! Slap! Slap! Slap!

"Alright, man, alright!" Wameek hurled up at him, eyes blinking and tearing.

"She was a kid, Wa, just a lil' fuckin' girl," Malik stood erect, nostrils expanding and shrinking. His chest swelled and fell, fists clenched tightly. He had it in him to beat his ass to death but he'd keep that urge at bay. After taking a deep breath, he ran his hand down his face and exhaled. Outstretching his hand, he pulled him up to his feet and wiped his bloody mouth with the lower inside of his shirt. Next, he gave him a brotherly hug and kissed him on the cheek. "I'm sorry, bro, I'm sorry. I shouldn't have hit chu."

"I'm sorry too, man, I fucked up. It won't happen again. I promise." He swore with a convincing look in his eyes, looking sorrowful.

"It's okay," he patted him on his back. Wameek stared over his shoulder at Fear during he and his brother's embrace, smiling with a wicked scowl. The look he had on his face was like I got this nigga wrapped around my finger.

Big brother kissed younger brother on the forehead and held his head against his for a time, apologizing once again.

"Y'all help me get this body wrapped up and put into the truck of the car." Fear told them, tucking his .9mm on his waistline. "I'll dispose of her while y'all clean shit up around here."

"Cool." Malik responded. "Listen, about..." he went to apologize about his threatening to shoot him but he stopped him.

"Don't even worry about it, family, let's put this work in so we don't have to stress getting jammed up on no murder beef."

"I heard that shit." Wameek nodded, garnering stern looks of Shut the fuck up from his family. He cleared his throat and muted himself real quick.

"After this ,we gon' breeze for a while to lay low," Malik informed Fear. "I'm pretty sure yo' dumb ass was seen at the club tonight with old girl, right?" Wameek hung his head shamefully and nodded. This enraged him again. He felt hotness around his ears and neck. "Fuckin' stupid!" He kicked him in the thigh and when he doubled over, he slapped fire out of his ass.

Slap!

"Aww, bro, what the fuck?" He grimaced, rubbing his stinging cheek.

"Shut up! Shut the fuck up! Shut it!" He gritted, shaking a crooked finger in his face. Wameek shut his mouth with the quickness. "Y'all come on." He waved them on as he headed toward the bedroom where the teenage girl's dead body was.

The fellas wrapped the body up in a floor rug, duct-taped it up and dumped it into the trunk of Malik's ride. While he went to dispose of the corpse, they got busy showering and dressing. Afterwards, they ate breakfast and waited for their little cousin's return. Not long after there was a knock at the door, Malik hopped to his feet to answer it. As soon as Fear stepped through the door they slapped hands and embraced.

"Glad you made it back, reli," Malik told him, patting him on the back.

"Me too. Let me get these bags for y'all, fam, make sho' this bitch locked up 'fore y'all make y'all outro." He grabbed their luggage and made his way outside, the bright rays of the sun creating a florescent glow around him. He'd just finished placing the luggage into the trunk of Malik's Challenger when he and his brother were approaching.

"Is that everything?" Malik asked, stepping out onto the sidewalk.

"Yeah." Fear nodded, slamming the trunk shut.

"Alright, my nigga, the kingdom is yours until the king returns."

They did a complex handshake and pounded the B against their chests.

"Don't fuck up." He shot his little cousin a serious expression, raising his eyebrow and pointing his finger.

"I won't." His eyes came across Wameek whose eye was twitching while he was sneering at him. He didn't pay him any mind though.

Bitch made ass nigga, he thought shaking his head. A nigga always had to take action if they wanted to show him that they were 'Bout It.

Malik tapped his brother and said, "Ain't chu gone say goodbye to yo' relative, fool?"

"Man, fuck that lil' nigga." He shot daggers at him.

Fear smirked and gave him the middle finger.

"This nigga," Malik exhaled shaking his head. He looked back to their cousin. "Alright, fam, we're outta here."

The Simpson brothers hopped into Malik's Dodge Challenger and it fired up, smoke fogging out of its chrome tail pipes. Fear patted the roof of the whip and Wameek pulled off. He stood on the curb watching the brake lights of the hood favorite until it had disappeared up the block. He then stepped to the telephone booth and dropped two quarters into the coin slot. He glanced over his shoulders occasionally as he listened to the line ring.

"9-1-1 what's your emergency?"

"Yes, I just saw these two guys load a dead body into the trunk of their car," Fear spoke into the phone, sounding like a real life civilian in panic. "I got the model of the car and the license plate…a silver Dodge Challenger, license plate Top Dawg." The operator was saying something when he hung the telephone up in her face. Without any time to waste, he darted across the street and into the front passenger seat of Italia's BMW. As soon as the door slammed shut she pulled off, speeding trying to catch up with the brothers. She caught up to Wameek and Malik and followed them two lanes over and four cars behind. Fear heard the police cruiser sirens and looked up in the rearview mirror: there were three cruisers coming up, red and blue lights spinning and blaring. The cars boxed the Challenger in and then the cop barked over his transceiver for the driver to pull over. The Challenger stopped and the doors flew open. The siblings came out, both armed with them head bussas, they lifted their heaters just as the police were.

Boc! Boc! Boc!

Pop! Pop! Pop! Pop! Pop! Pop!

Malik went down first, grabbing his chest and howling as he crashed to the sidewalk. Wameek was just behind him red dots expanding on his white T-shirt before he lay stretched out in the middle of the street with the occasional car flying past. Fear listened as his cousins groaned in agony. The police engaged them cautiously with their guns on the ready, dying for a reason to unleash some kill shots. Hastily, the brothers were turned on their stomachs and handcuffed. They were made to lie in the street bleeding until an ambulance arrived. Seeing Wameek and Malik being placed on gurneys and rolled towards the ambulance caused Fear's lips to form a smile. He stuck his pinky finger at the corner of his mouth and whistled, stealing their attention. Their heads snapped in his direction. They realized that it was him that had set them up. They started hurling insults and spitting at him. He waved in return and pulled off.

One of the police officers popped the trunk while the others stood at the rear. Once they heard the thunk they lifted the trunk and feasted their eyes on what was stored inside.

"Sweet Jesus, poor kid." A blonde haired policeman shook his head, seeing Tamara's lifeless form.

"What cha got?" Myers asked from where he was posted up by his police cruiser.

"Come check this out." He waved him over, face balled up because he was sickened by the sight.

The quartet of uniforms stood at the trunk admiring what was inside. Using a pen, one of them lifted the gun that Fear used to kill O'Connor out of the trunk as well as the one that was used to murder his family.

The officer whistled thinking of all of the time the Simpson brothers was going to get for what they'd found inside of their trunk along with the dead body of the teenage girl.

"You guys are fucked with no Vaseline," Myers told the twins.

"Fuck you talking about?" Wameek snapped angrily.

"LaSalle, Finkle, bring those two shit-birds over here," Blonde told the other officers. The Simpson brothers were pulled roughly to their feet and escorted to the rear of the car. Their eyes grew as wide as saucers once they saw

Tamara and the two handguns that were stashed at the corner of the trunk.

"What the fuck?!" Malik couldn't believe his eyes.

"We didn't put that mothafucka there!" Wameek shouted.

"Yeah, I just bet," One of the police officers said.

Malik and Wameek got twenty five years to life inside of a California state prison.

Fear felt bad having gotten Malik involved in the trap that he'd set for Wameek but he had to play it smart. He knew that the oldest twin would be gunning for him if he ever found out that he had set his brother up so he had to do what he had to do. He looked at it as killing two birds with one stone. Besides, he'd originally planned on murking them both out, but ruled that the punishment would be too sever when it came to Malik whose hands were clean of Tamara's blood.

"You okay, baby?" Italia looked over at Fear who was staring out of the front passenger side window, watching the city streets pass him by. He grasped her freehand and looked to her with a smile.

"I'm good, sweetheart." He kissed her hand and went back to staring out of the window.

With the twins out of the way, Fear went on to expand the blossoming empire he'd inherited. He bought more drugs, more guns, and employed more soldiers. He applied a chokehold to the game and didn't let it from out of his grasp. Now don't get it fucked up. He was winning before, but never like this. Things were going to be different because he was the top dawg now. This would be a new regime. He would go on to reach another plateau with the shit he was lying down. He got respect from both the old school and the new school hustlers. They saluted him and his accomplishments and at the same time they stayed the fuck out of his way. They were made well aware of how he got down for his and treaded lightly around him.

CHAPTER TWELVE
2010

Fear sent the bosses a kite letting them know that The Bluudlow Brothers had been executed. The million dollars he received for their murders was stored in a safe place. Being that he was in the street life he knew that it was better to play it safe than to be sorry later on. That money was going to be used to pay off lawyers, witnesses, and if need be, a couple of hardheads who weren't afraid to put that work in. Later that night, Fear decided to take Italia for a night out on the town. They went on a horse and carriage ride and ate at a five star restaurant called Raphael's, which was located out in North Hollywood. They were enjoying their meals and expensive wine, indulging in friendly conversation. It wasn't until Italia started rubbing her bare foot up and down his crotch that things got hot and steamy. On the spot, Fear paid for their meal and dropped a tip. He grabbed her hand and was out of the door. His lady had him on fire and he couldn't wait to get home so she could put him out. Now here they were kissing slow and sensually as they undressed one another, allowing their garments to fall at their feet in piles. Fear licked up her throat to underneath her chin, traveling downward gently biting on her neck. Coming to her chest he placed kisses on it and grabbed her plentiful breasts, mashing them together. His tongue traced her areolas causing her nipples to stand erect. His warm, juicy mouth engulfed her left breast and sucked on it thirstily, making murmuring noises as he did so. When he moved to the consumption of her next breast, she threw her head back, eyes shut as she licked her top lip. She could feel his hot breath and the moistness of his mouth on her as he devoured her bosoms. Sliding down and kneeling to her navel, he licked the arch that formed the V that lead to her vagina. Right After he was biting softly on it and then slicking it with his tongue. Once he moved to the other hip, he did the exact same thing. Only he was rubbing his hand up and down her inner thigh, feeling the warm comfort that her coochie provided. He took one of her legs and propped it on top of the dresser, getting down on his knees beneath her. He admired that beautiful pussy of hers. It was practically bald besides the thin landing strip of hair it was styled with.

Fear held onto the thigh of the leg of hers that was planted firmly on the floor, before jabbing at her asshole with his hot, slick tongue. This action drew hisses from her and caused her to wince, eyes still shut. He tongue slid over her taint, in between her pussy lips and stopped at her clit. He flicked it with his tongue before sucking on it.

"Ooooh, aawww," she whined and grabbed the back of his neck, trying to force his face deeper inside of her. His breaths were short and husky as he handled his. She feeling him, her big toes pointing while the others balled like fingers were clarification of this. He slightly smiled knowing that he was pleasing his woman. This was just the beginning though. Now it was time to bring his fingers into play. First, he slid in his pointer finger which startled her because she wasn't expecting them. In a slow rhythm which he eventually sped up, he finger fucked her, his mouth and fingers working together in harmony to bring her an explosive orgasm.

"Mmmmm," He murmured as he ate that pussy like it had a cherry Star Burst trapped inside that he was trying to get. Before he knew it, she was twitching and her river of love came spilling from between her legs, running down his hand and dripping off of his knuckles. He took his fingers from out of her and crawled upon the bed, alongside her. With lustful eyes, he watched her suck her very own juices from his fingers causing his dick to become engorged with his blood. Its width and length reached its full potential, its head looking like an overgrown mushroom tip. Italia sucked his fingers and jacked his meat, multitasking. He threw his head back and enjoyed her sexual prowess. Horny as all hell, he took his fingers from her lips and brought his grown man toward her lips. As soon as her hot, salivating mouth married his rod he moaned like a little bitch. Squeezing his eyes shut and biting down on his bottom lip, his worked his hips and jabbed her mouth. Her gagging turned him on and he pumped faster, looking down at her handling her business and sweeping her long hair out of her face.

"Haaaa! Shit! Sssssss, yes, get it, momma. Suck it, yeah, suck it just like that." He spoke in a hoarse voice, eyes fluttering and lips peeling apart.

"MmmmMmmmm." Her eyes were closed as she sucked and jerked his meat.

"Sssssss, ah, sssss, ahh!" He licked his lips and pumped even faster. "Yeah, that it."

Fear allowed his lady to pamper his swipe until he found himself about to nut. Right then, he withdrew his steel from her jaws and smacked her ass. Face down ass up, he gave her instructions as he positioned himself behind her. Italia did just like he had ordered, her face was buried into the pillow and her apple shaped at was tooted up in the air, giving him the view of the most beautiful pussy he had ever seen. Looking at her glistening hole caused his shit to grow even harder. He could wait to slide off in her. Grabbing the beginning of his dick, he inched up behind her aiming its swollen head for the entrance of her pleasure zone. He planted one masculine vein riddled hand on her left buttock and squeezed it, meat seeping between his fingers. They both his hissed as he slowly filled up her pink cavern, enjoying the snug fit of her vagina's walls. He smacked her left buttocks and gripped it with his freehand, zeroing in on his diamond hardness. Pleasure was written across his face as well as her as he pushed and pulled his himself out of her creamy center. The greater the sensation their sexing brought, the harder he pumped her, gritting and fighting back his urge to let loose inside of her.

"Ahhhh, fuck, babe, this shit bomb, the pussy all of that!" His eyes were narrowed into white slits and his mouth was hanging open. He plowed into her with vigor, building up a sweat. His body shined all over. He angled his head and sucked his lips inwards, continuing his massaging of her treasure.

"Uh! Uh! Uh!" her eyes were squeezed shut and her mouth formed a tight line, she held his knees as he smashed her from the back. The sound of her big old ass clashing with his stubble mound, made her run wet and caused her clit to throb without mercy. This nigga was driving her wild.

"Ssssss, I'm finna cum! I'm finna cum, baby." His voice grew deeper as it always did when he was fucking and the P was superb,

"Bust in me, sssss, I wanna feel all of that warm shit shoot up in me!" she whined and squared her jaws, face shiny from perspiration.

He threw his head back and gripped her ass tighter, thrusting harder and faster. "Grrrr, here I come!" he looked down at his dick, sliding it all of the way inside of her until nothing but his nut sack was dangling out of her. He grimaced and his hips twitched, filling up her P with his hot creamy lather and then watching it run down her legs. A smile formed across her face, loving his warm children spilling inside of her womb.

Fear collapsed beside her in bed breathing hard, his chest jumping up and down. His entire form was glistening. Italia crawled over to him, licking his nipples and kissing on his chest. He listened to her mmmm's and shut his eyes, biting down on his inner jaw. A smile spread across his lips.

"Sssss, you tryna go for round two, huh?" He asked with his eyes shut.

"Uh huh," She replied between licks and kisses. "You down for one more?"

"I don't know maybe. That first one killed me off." He chuckled.

She sat up in bed with her hands on her hips, a crooked smile on her face. "Old man can't hang, huh?"

He busted up laughing. "Old man? I'll show you old man."

"Take it easy, pops, I don't want chu to throw yo' back out." He patted his chest and sashayed toward the bathroom.

"Ahhh, that was cold." He laughed aloud. Propping his fist against the side of his head, he watched her cakes jiggle on her short journey. Italia got two washcloths soapy and wet with hot water. She planted her foot upon the commode's lid and scrubbed her pussy, wiping her legs in process as well. Once she was done, she returned to the bedroom and cleaned Fear up. Having gotten that out of the way, she cuddled up beside him in bed making plans for them to take a shower together later on.

Fear lay with his hands behind his head, staring up at the ceiling. His eyes were glassy and a disturbed look was on his face. Worry lines came across Italia's forehead as she looked up at him from his chest where she'd laid her head for comfort, listening to the rhythm of his steady heart beat.

"What's wrong, baby?" She asked concerned.

He shook his head, while continuing to stare up at the ceiling. "Ain't shit, I'm straight."

She kept her eyes on him, trying to read him. That's when it dawned on her the possibility of what it was that was riding down on his emotions.

"Is it your father?"

That was it. As soon as she mentioned his old man, he shut his eyes to thwart off the tears that had quickly accumulated in his eyes. Clenching his jaws, he fought back the urge to breakdown and cry. He wanted so badly for her to hold him and allow him to sob in her arms. Although he desired this, he wouldn't allow it. His woman had to look at her king and know that he was the epitome of strength and sophistication. To him to display such emotion again would make him appear as weak. It was bad enough that he'd lost it at his father's funeral. He'd be damned if he'd lose it in front of her again. When he peeled his eyelids back open again, the pain that residing in them was gone. He turned over in bed to his queen.

"I'm good, baby." Fear stroked Italia's chin with his thumb before kissing her delicately on the lips, staring into her eyes lovingly. Hearing vibrating and ringing over his shoulder, he rolled over in bed and picked up his cellular from off the dresser. His face frowned with a questioning expression when he saw Hahn 's name on the display. For as long as they knew one another the old man had never called him. Hell, far as he knew he didn't own a TV let alone a telephone, so he was curious as to know why he'd suddenly decided to call him. If Hahn wasn't studying martial arts, he was meditating and/or keeping his nose buried inside of some book. He was as health and as strong as bull. That was saying a lot for a man his age. At seventy five, Fear was sure that his master could whoop any twenty, twenty-five year olds ass.

"Master Hahn, is everything alright?" Fear spoke into his cell, sitting up in bed and slipping on his pajama pants.

"Yes, everything is fine," he finally spoke.

There was a long, awkward silence between student and teacher.

"Umm, are you sure?" His brows furrowed, wondering what was eating the man that he admired almost as much as his own father. Although he knew that his mentor wasn't big on expressing his emotions, he hoped that he would give his something to let him know where his head was at.

Silence.

"Master Hahn ?" Fear stood up and walked over to the terrace, sliding open the glass door. Cool air rushed inside and ruffled the curtains. The draft felt good against his half naked body. Silence. "Master Hahn , are you there?" the groove in his forehead deepened as he pressed the device closer to his mouth, clutching it. The old man went into a nasty coughing fit making him sound like he was about to chuck up a lung. That's when it dawned on him that his master was sick, terminally sick. Silence again. He shut his eyelids and when he pulled them back open they were glassy. "You got cancer." Everything grew still and quiet. He listened closely for his mentor's response and then it happened. He hung up.

"Is everything, okay, baby?" Italia called out from the bedroom.

Fear took a deep breath before responding. "No. Hahn 's dying."

"What?" She slipped on her panties and a baby T, her pretty manicured toes stepped out onto the terrace where she found her man with his back to her. "Has he been injured or something?" She questioned with general concern in her voice.

"It's cancer." He was on the verge of tears as he took in the full scope of the well lit city in the sea of darkness, head moving from left to right. It was beautiful and reminded him of the view inside of the suite back in Las Vegas. Italia embraced him from behind and laid her head against his back, shutting her eyes and inhaling his scent.

"I'm sorry, babe, I'm terribly, terribly sorry." She took her head from his back and kissed him tenderly on his spine. He shut his eyes and tears jetted down his cheeks. He quickly wiped his face with a curled finger and the back of his hand. His cellular rang and vibrated then. Looking down at the display, he saw Big Sexy and answered it. There exchange was brief and he was disconnecting the call shortly thereafter. "Who was that?"

"Sex," he replied, turning around to her. Although he was no longer crying she could see the hurt dwelling inside of his eyes. Her lover was in great emotional pain and she couldn't quite imagine how he must have felt. He'd lost his father and the man who was like a surrogate father to him all within a matter of weeks. Those events had to be tearing him apart inside. She wanted so badly to relieve him of all that he was going through at the time, but nothing short of a miracle could do that and she wasn't God. So a loving, caressing touch against the side of his face would have to do along with an I love you to accompany it.

"I love you." She stared deep into his eyes, gently stoking the side of his face.

"I love you, too." He answered, closing his eyes and holding her hand against his cheek as she tried to sooth his pain. They stood out there in the terrace for a time basking in the moment before he broke it. "I've gotta get dressed. Sex will be here in a minute."

"Alright." They kissed and he ducked back off inside. She watched him move back and forth across their bedroom, buckling up a pair of Levi's 501s and sliding on some Timberland boots. He stashed a Glock on his waistline and slipped the strap of a MP-5 over his shoulder, before slipping a poncho over his head. He threw on the hoodie of the poncho and faced the mirror that sat over the dresser. In his reflection he saw Italia sitting on the bed still observing him.

"I'll be back before you know it." He kissed her tenderly on the forehead and headed for the doorway, only stopping once she'd called him back. "Yeah?"

"Is there anything that you're afraid of?"

"Only one." He held up a finger.

"Well, what?" She sat up in bed, anticipating his answer.

"Losing you."

"You don't ever have to worry about losing me. Nothing but the cold hands of death could pry me from your side."

"And that's what I'm afraid of." When he said this it stunned her. She didn't know exactly how to reply so he continued, "I'll be back soon, okay?"

"Okay." She nodded.

"I don't want chu staying here worrying, it will drive you crazy."

"I'm not. I'ma go to the store to get a few things to cook for dinner tomorrow."

"Good."

She shut her eyes as he kissed her lips and then her forehead. He pressed his forehead against hers and closed his eyes for a moment as she held on to his hand. She then pressed her face against his torso, taking a deep inhalation of his scent. If this was taken be their last time together she always wanted to reflect back and relive the moment in time. He still had his eyes closed as well. Before he entered the killing field, he would commit this moment to his memory, using it as a reason to get back home. Fear kissed his lady on the mouth giving her just a little tongue before turning to leave. He stopped short being that she still had a hold on the tail end of his poncho. Turning around, he took her hand and kissed it, making his way toward the door. Again, he'd almost crossed the threshold out of the door when she called him back. He turned around with an eyebrow rose like, What's up?

Teary eyed and worry drawn on her face, she said, "I love you."

"Dido," He replied, stepping off to usher some mark ass niggaz to their final destinations.

Later that night

The Bar Fly was dimly lit provided by the illumination of the lights above the pool tables and well lit Juke Box. The establishment was scarcely occupied. There was a couple of regulars sitting at the bar savoring the taste of hard liquor and taking the occasional swigs of their beers. The rest of the patrons were at the pool tables partaking in friendly games or bets. They all seemed to be enjoying themselves and having a good old time. The environment was welcoming save for the shady characters taking up the opposite end of the place. There wasn't a soul on their end of the bar that wasn't brethren, and no one was invited besides their own.

"Bitch ass niggaz took out my peoples. Nah, fuck that they gotta pay us in blood, ya feel me?" Killa Jay said sharpening his pool stick with a blue cube, his jeweled hand twisting back and forth. He was a chubby cat of a brown hue. He rocked a black doo-rag with flap, a platinum and diamond grill and a Sean Jean sweat suit. Over it he wore several thin gold necklaces. This was the leader of The Untouchables. A five man collective whose sole purpose was to murder, each killer was more deadly than the last.

"You know who did that?" BoBo asked, leaning over the table to take his shot. He was a tall, skinny nigga who sported his hair in a tapered afro.

"Word on the street is that it was that nigga Fear and his man," Snoop spoke up. He was light skinned, chubby dude that rocked his hair in cornrows.

"Who, Big Sexy?" Killa Jay's forehead creased.

"Yeah that's his faggot ass." One of the goons butted into the conversation.

"Big Sexy?" Another one of the goons laughed. "Yo, hold up, what type of grown ass man calls himself Big Sexy?"

"Laugh all you won't, but that fat ass nigga there ain't nothin' to play games with, trust." Killa Jay's eyes were glassy and disturbed as he took a swig from his Heineken. He wasn't afraid of man breathing but he knew how Big Sexy and Fear got down for theirs. They were all killers and respected their peers.

"Should I be shaking in my boots?" the goon asked, looking like Ain't nan nigga pumping fear into my heart.

"Nah, lil' nigga, you bet not be afraid. The squad ain't pussy we fuck it." He sat the beer down on the edge of the pool table and made to take the shot. "I'm telling you not to underestimate this man. He isn't some nickel and dime corner hustler, he'll bust ya muddafuckin'head wide open."

The goon shrugged. "So, my guns go off, too. What chu saying?"

"Fuck!"Killa Jay cursed and slammed the butt of his stick into the floor, pissed. A line etched across his forehead. He looked up at the newest member of their alliance. "What I'm sayin' shut the fuck up the next time you see me about to take my shot. I got five stacks ridin' on this game." He flicked a hundred dollar bill up from the pile of dead presidents on the edge of the pool table.

"Yo, who you talkin' too?" He gritted, eyebrows arching.

With an indention on his forehead, the chubby man turned around in a 380 degree turn looking around. He thought he may have heard wrong because he just knew that the little mothafucka wasn't talking to him. "My nigga, fuck you think you talkin' to?" his eyes darkened and he clenched his jaws, hand moving toward the bulge on his waistline.

Off to the side by the bar, the bartender and owner of the establishment, Nigel, who was cleaning out a mug with a rag, sat the glass down and dipped below the bar, grasping a Mossberg pump. He racked it and whispered something to the only waitress on duty that night.

The goon kicking shit at Killa Jay went to spit something disrespectful from his big lips but his brother stepping in between him halted that move.

"Moody, gon' and pull the truck up out front, man, we'll be out in a minute." Watts gave him a stern look, pushing the car keys into his chest.

Moody was locked into an intense gaze with the leader of his squad. There was murdered glinting in both of their eyes, their hearts thumping and trigger fingers itching. In a split second they could get it cracking out that bitch. The rest of the members of The Untouchables eyes were shifty, going back and forth between their head honcho and the young boy. They wouldn't get involved. Nah, the last one standing once those guns rung would be the winner of the dispute.

"Bruh, gon'." Watts frowned and pointed to the exit, grabbing his little brother by the arm and turning him toward the door. He grudgingly went along but he kept his eyes on Killa Jay. The youngster was steaming and dying to get active with that ass. Truthfully, he didn't feel like the pie face killer should be That Nigga In Charge. See, he felt it should be him helming their thing; because in his opinion, old boy was pushing forty and was washed up. Their crew needed new blood to lead the way and he was just that guy. "Get the fuck on!" he stabbed his finger at the door.

Moody snatched his arm away and stomped off like a five year old throwing a tantrum. His brother watched him until he disappeared through the exit door before turning around to Killa Jay. Wrinkles formed across his forehead and the bridge of his nose. He patted the leader of their gang on his shoulder and gripped it, taking a deep breath.

"Sorry about that, KJ." He apologized.

"No sweat." Killa Jay said to him before turning around to the pool table continuing his game, lining his pool stick up with the white Q-ball. The tip of the stick jabbed at the ball toying with the thought of hitting it. Blaq! The white ball struck the red striped ball and it dropped inside of the corner pocket. After making that shot, Watts patted him on the back and he rounded the table, positioning himself to take the next shot.

Forty five minutes later

The Untouchables came staggering out of The Bar Fly tipsy and laughing their asses off. The Excursion was parked curbside waiting for them with Moody behind the wheel, its windows pulsating from 2pac's Hail Mary.

BoBo came down from his laughter and knocked on the black tinted window of the enormous truck. "Yo, Moody, open up, man." He grabbed the door handle and looked back at his niggaz, chuckling. They were coming around to the other side of the SUV. "Y'all niggaz stupid." He shook his head and turned back around to the front passenger door. "Moody, man, open up!" he said louder.

"What's up?" Watts frowned.

"Yo bro playin' and shit. I'm ready to take it home shit." He cupped his hands around the glass and tried to peer inside. He strained his eyes trying to see what the young nigga was doing inside but he couldn't see him.

By this time ,all of the fellas were complaining about having to wait to get inside of the truck.

Knock! Knock! Knock! Knock!

"Open up the fuckin' doors, lil' nigga!" Killa Jay's brows furrowed as he rapped on the window furiously.

"I got it." Watts said, trying to move him aside, but he snatched away.

"Nah, yo' folks had this ass whipping a long time comin', fam. Tonight is the night." He whipped his tool off of his waistline and struck the window with the butt of it. With each strike the glass cracked into a cobweb more and more until it eventually gave. Killa Jay jumped back when the black glass fell and rained out on the street. He narrowed his eyelids trying not to get any of the broken pieces in his eyes. When he looked up, he saw the side of Moody's face mashed up against the steering wheel. There were two black holes in his forehead which were dripping blood. His eyes were as big as tennis balls and his mouth was ajar. The driver side of the windshield had two holes in it and they both were cracked into a spider's web.

Killa Jay wore a shocked expression on his face as he stepped back, crossing himself in the sign of the crucifix.

"Mothafucka! Mothafuckkkkaz!" Watts hollered out having seen his brother murdered out. His eyes welled up with tears and shot down his cheeks. He drew his burner and the rest of the homies did as well. "You're dead, you hear me? You. Are. Fuckin'. Dead!" He said at the top of his lungs, veins bulging out of his neck and temples.

Killa Jay, Watts, BoBo and the other homie ,Snoop, heads were on a swivel, looking all around for who could have done Moody like that. While they were looking all around 2pac's Hail Mary continued to play on, while patrons from The Bar Fly crowded the establishment's doorway gazing on.

I ain't a killer but don't push me

Revenge is like the sweetest joy next to gettin pussy
Picture paragraphs unloaded, wise words bein quoted
Peeped the weakness in the rap game and sewed it
Bow down, pray to God hoping that he's listenin
Seein niggaz comin for me, to my diamonds, when they
glistenin
Now pay attention, rest in peace father
I'm a ghost in these killin fields

"Snoop, kill that stereo!" Killa Jay ordered with authority. His homeboy did what he was ordered and did as he was told and joined back up with his crew.

"You think whoeva did this is still out here?" BoBo asked Killa Jay in a hushed tone, waving his burner around like the rest of his squad.

"I don't know, but if they are they're dead! I didn't much care for Moody but he was an Untouchable." He swung his gun from left to right, dying to let some hot ones go in the direction that the threat presented its self.

All you could see was the cold white breaths of The Untouchables as they moved around, chests heaving up and down. Their adrenaline was pumping and their hearts were thumping behind their left pecks. The patrons still looked on from the doorway anxious to see how this entire situation was going to play its self out. The night was as silent as the grave. The only thing that could be heard was the slight sound of the killers' breathing. That was until there was the sound of a motorcycle revving up.

Vroom! Vroom! Vroom! Vroom!

The loud noise cracked the silence and they whipped around ready to bust a nigga'z body up. When they saw that it was just a Harley Davidson, they relaxed a little and that's when they heard the sound of gravel being crunched under sneakers. They went to move and rapid gunfire came fast and fierce. A man in a hood, whose face was in the dark from the shade of it, stepped from out of the alley and off of the curb. Hands slightly shaking as he let loose with a MP-5, sweeping it back and forth. The hot lead nearly cut them all in half. They threw their heads back screaming and their bodies bent at funny angles, feeling that heat pass in and out of them. The cold blooded killers fell out in the street blood and twisted, guns clacking to the asphalt. The hooded man braced his machine gun with both gloved hands, his head moving about as he looked over the bodies. The chests of BoBo and Watts were still rising and falling as they both moaned in agony. He looked over his shoulder and saw Killa Jay limping away and holding his sides having gotten shot in them both. The stranger in the hood withdrew a Glock .40 and walked upon the survivors, pointing his weapon down at their foreheads.

Bloc! Bloc!

Their brains splattered against their street when the hollow tip bullets slammed into their skulls, finishing them off. He looked up and seen Killa Jay getting further away from him. With that in mind, he looked to the doorway of The Bar Fly and saw the patrons staring at him. When he lifted his MP-5 in their direction, they ducked back inside and slammed the door shut in a hurry. Having gotten the witnesses out of the way, he slipped the strap of his machinegun over his head. Listening to the police cruisers sirens heading to his location, he started off after the leader of what the streets had claimed was The World's Most Dangerous Crew. Glock at his side, he moved in for the kill whistling Dixie like murder was just another day at the office for him.

"Oh, shit!" Killa Jay looked over his shoulder and saw the stranger in pursuit. This renewed his stamina, and made him limp along even faster. His breathing growing huskier the further he moved. He found that his forehead had grown sweaty as well as his palms. He was scared as hell.

This was as close as he had ever been to death. The nigga had grown too use to being on the other side of the gun.

"Haa! Haa! Haa! Haa! Haa!" He constantly looked over his shoulder with a pair of big, terrified eyes. Turning his head back around, he wiped his perspiring forehead with the back of his hand. That's when he felt the calf of his good leg explode, causing him to howl in pain and drop in the middle of the street. Glancing over his shoulder, he saw the nigga in the hood speed walking toward him. He nearly shitted in his boxer briefs seeing the man so close. The son of a bitch looked more like The Grim Reaper than someone wearing a hood being as he could only see darkness where his face should have been.

Killa Jay winced as he turned himself over slowly, throwing up his hand trying to plead for his life. The Glock came up firing and empty shell cases flew out of it in blurs. Bloc! One through the heart. Bloc! Bloc! Two to the head. With the deed done, homie strolled off whistling and tucked his thang on his waistline. He stopped at a white brick fence which was a mess with other graffiti. Pulling out a can of spray paint, he shook it up real good and brought it to the fence. Sssssssss! Sssssssss! Sssssssss! The red spray paint ran like blood from open wounds as he wrote what he had in mind, steadily whistling. Taking a step back, he took a good look at his work. Satisfied, he tossed the spray paint into the gutter and strolled off just as police cruisers were invading the block. When law enforcement finally made it on the scene the first thing they noticed were the sprawled dead bodies of Killa Jay and his niggaz. Written on the wall was The Untouchables with the U and N crossed out, The Touchables.

CHAPTER THIRTEEN
2010
Sometime later that night

"Honey, I'm home!" Fear smiled coming through the door of his condo, closing it shut behind him. He journey into the kitchen where he opened the refrigerator and retrieved a Heineken, popping the cap off of it. After tossing the bottle opener onto the counter, he took a long drink, his throat rolling up and down as he did so. Wiping off his chin with the back of his fist, he wandered through the house calling his lady's name. "Baybeee, where are you, sweetness?" He took a swig of his beer and hiked up the steps, one foot at a time. Reaching his bedroom he flipped on the light-switch and found his bed in the exact condition he'd left it. "Guess she hasn't made it back yet," he said to himself shrugging and moving forth. As soon as he crossed the threshold into his bedroom, his cell phone rang and vibrated inside of his pocket of his jeans. He dipped into the pocket and retrieved it, looking down at the screen seeing Italia on it. A smile crept upon his face. He was none the wiser to the man that had stepped into the doorway behind him, his shadow darkening the carpet. The floor creaked when the man lumbered forth, but by the time Fear realized that he wasn't alone it was already too late. Something hard and heavy had slammed against the back of his head, dropping him where he stood. He hit the floor with a thud, lying on the side of his face with the beer running out onto the floor while he lay unconscious. His cell phone lay beside him with Italia still on its screen as it rung continuously, until finally, a missed call came up.

A half an hour later

Fear sat with his head hung and bound to an iron chair by rope. A dirty, yellowing light bulb hanging from a string illuminated him from above, flies circling it. The bulb flickered from time to time like it was threatening to go out. Fear's captor, a brown skinned man with a muscular build, stood off to the side, smoke wafting around him as he indulged in his habit. He observed him as if he were a wild animal inside of a cage at the zoo. The man dropped a cigarette at his sneaker and mashed it out, blowing smoke out of his nostrils and mouth.

"Hey, wake up!" He yelled at Fear. When he didn't get a response, he swung his hand across his face.

Smack!

"I said wake your black ass up, nigga!" Spittle jumped from off his lips, palm stinging from the attack. He continued his assault, only more viciously.

Smack!

Smack!

His nostrils flared and his chest rose and fell rapidly. He bored down at his shorter man with contempt. Closing his eyes and taking deep breaths to calm himself, he disappeared into the shadows of the darkened basement. When he returned, he was toting a tin bucket full of water. He stopped before Fear, cocked the tin bucket back, and splashed water into his face. Fear's head shot up and he gasped for air.

"Haaaa!" He sounded like someone had held his head underwater and waited until the last minute to let him up. Water cascaded down his face as his eyelids fluttered and he took in his surroundings. Once his vision finally came into focus, he got a good look at the cat standing before him.

"Fuck are you, man?" Fear asked with an attitude, his voice resonating throughout the space.

"I'm Detective Broli."

Fear tried to move, but the rope held him fast. He looked down and saw that he was bound tightly to an iron chair. When he saw this, his brows furrowed and wrinkles formed across the beginning of his nose. What the fuck is this? He wondered what the hell he was restrained to a chair for.

He looked up and asked, "What's this shit about?"

"You," Broli answered. "I've been watching you this past few years. You've made an insane amount of money pushing crack, kingpin. That's tax free money, so the Feds aren't seeing one red cent of that. So I figure why don't I step in and play Uncle Sam? From now on, I want fifty percent of your take. Your workers, your lawyer fees, anyone else who may have put the lean on you, that's your business. Their pay comes outta your end. I don't give a damn, fuck you pay me. We understand one another?"

Fear threw his head back laughing. I mean, he actually had tears forming in his eyes he was laughing so hard.

"Hahahahahaha, ooooh, shit," Fear came down from his laughter, chuckling. "You should do stand up, my nigga. You're the next Red Foxx. Whoo! Me? Getting muscled for my empire? That will be the day a nigga applies the pressure game on me and I fold. Fuck I look like nigga?" He harped up a glob of phlegm and spit on his sneaker, glaring up at him like What the fuck you gone do?

Broli frowned and clenched his jaws, looking down at the nasty goo on the side of his sneaker. He kicked his foot until most of the phlegm went flying across the way. He felt himself getting angry, but he quickly caught himself, a sinister smile across his lips making him resemble the devil himself.

"What do you look like you ask?" Fear watched closely as he popped the trunk of his car and removed a briefcase. Closing the trunk shut, he advanced in Fear's direction and sat the briefcase on his lap, popping its locks. He lifted its lid and removed a stack of black and white photographs. Slamming the briefcase shut, he laid the photos on top of it and went through them, one by one.

Broli looked up at Fear who was still smiling from his laughing earlier. Both of the men were smiling, but it was the crooked detective that held the trump card.

"Let's see how long you're wearing that smile of yours, asshole."

With each photograph that Broli revealed, the smile on Fear's face grew smaller and smaller until it had vanished. Fear felt his heart slide deep down into the pit of his stomach and wither like a dying leaf. The black and white photographs were of Fear participating in the murders of The Bluudlow Brothers, The Untouchables, and purchasing large shipments of weapons. Broli had him by the balls and was squeezing them, tighter and tighter. "I get the feeling that you've changed your mind."

Fear sat there with his head hung, shaking it. He shoulders rose and fell as he took deep breaths, thinking long and hard.

"Fuuck, man, shit!" he screamed and stomped the floor. Afterwards, he shut his eyes briefly and took a couple more deep breaths, calming himself. "Alright," He began, looking up at the shady badge defeated. "How you wanna play this?"

Broli put his fist to his mouth and cleared his throat. "I'm glad you asked." He patted his leg and pulled up another iron chair, sitting down. "Fuck what I said earlier, that's too much hassle. I've gotta 'nough drug dealers on my payroll. What I want from you," as he spoke he jabbed him in the knee with his finger for emphasis. "is one million dollas in cold cash."

"One million dollars and I walk?" He looked him square in the eyes for any signs of his lying.

"One million dollas and I'll evenburn this here evidence in front of you." He held up the photographs.

"How do I know you're not lying? You've gotta gimmie yo' word."

Broli's face twisted with anger and he leaned forward. "Let's get something straight, mothafucka, I've gotta 'nough dirt to lock you away for three life times." He held up three fingers. "You aren't in any position to bargain. I ain't gotta give you notta goddamn thing!" He dropped the photos on top of the briefcase and sat back in his chair, folding his arms across his chest. "So what's it gonna be, kingpin? You gon' un-ass that cash or am I gon' have to slap some cold cuffs on yo' ass?"

"If I give you this money, that's it, I can go?" he asked to make sure, searching his eyes for truthfulness once again.

"One million dollars and you're a free man. And the evidence is all yours." He patted the briefcase.

"Okay. I'll take you where I stashed it, cut me loose."

"Alright then," Broli began, picking up the machete from the floor, getting upon his feet. "Just so you know, if you try anything, I'ma use this big bastard to behead yo' mothafucking ass. Got that?"

"Loud and clear, killa," he spoke with a no nonsense attitude. Broli stepped behind him and relieved him off his bondages, with one swift move of the rope. The severed rope hit the floor and Fear rose to his feet, massaging his wrists.

"The doors open. Get inside of the car." Broli pointed his machete at his whip. Fear went to move too fast for him and he drew his piece from its holster on his hip. The swift motion caused him to look over his shoulder, eyebrow raised. "Slow ya roll now."

"Relax. I ain't going nowhere." He retreated to the car with the dirty detective by his side. Broli forced him inside of the car on the front passenger side with his gun pressed into his ribs. After passing his hostage the keys, he cranked up the engine and pulled off.

Fifty five minutes later

Italia sat on the couch watching TV. The blue illumination of the screen shone on her face as she held the remote control in her hand, changing the channels. She was bored as hell and couldn't wait until her man got home. Hearing the keys jingling at the front door, she sat up straight and slid her gown off of her shoulder. A sexy smile apprehended her luscious lips and she turned toward the door, sliding up her nightwear so that her boo could get a good look at her inviting thigh. She was hoping to entice him and possibly get some dick that night. Her pussy had been twitching the past couple of hours and she was in dire need of some of that thug passion.

The front door came open and the smile fell from her lips seeing Broli standing behind her dude. As soon as he saw her, he pressed his banger further into Fear's back and gripped the collar of his shirt tighter. The look he shot her was like Scream and I'm going to do this nigga right here. She read him like a text message and complied. The beauty wasn't about to do anything that would jeopardize the life of her lover.

"Babe, what's going on?" She inquired; worry was etched across her face.

"Everything is going to be okay, sweetheart, he'll be outta here in no time. I just gotta pay 'em off so he can go." His eyes darted to their corners at Broli. "Ain't that right, Big Dawg?"

"Sho' ya right." His dangerous eyes focused on Italia, wishing she would do something foolish so that he could blow a hole in her man's back. He pulled a pair of handcuffs from his back and tossed them on the floor at Italia's bare feet. "Cuff yourself to the guard railing of the staircase." Once he was done watching her do as he'd ordered, he led her guy upstairs where he claimed he had the million dollars stashed. They found themselves inside of the master bedroom. Gun still on Fear, Broli was ordered to dump the pillows from out of the pillowcases. He was planning to use them to carry all of the loot he would be given.

"Open up the safe, nigga! Come on, you taking too fucking long!" He shoved him peevishly.

"I got this, chill out."

"Chill out?" He gave him the evil eye. Whack! He smacked him across the back of the skull with that steel, dropping him down to a knee. He grimaced, holding his hand to the back of his dome. When he glanced at his hand he saw that it was masked with blood which meant that a gash had opened up on his head. "Talk back again and I'ma put one in yo' spine, lil' nigga! Now find that safe and pop that bitch open!"

Gritting in pain, Fear opened the closet door and parted the clothes hanging upon the rod, granting a clear path to a solid steel, digital safe that was as tall and as wide as a door. When Broli seen the safe, he smiled and stared at it like it was love at first sight. "Open her up." He nudged Fear who was still holding the back of his head wincing. He punched in the combo and the door made a thunk, coming ajar. When he pulled open the door, Broli almost nutted in his jeans. There were eight shelves and there wasn't one of them that didn't have money on it. Every stack accounted for was secured by a rubber band. It was more than a million dollars here, two or three maybe, but definitely more. Broli passed the pillowcases to Fear and he started filling them up, making sure that he'd given him a million dollars. Once he was done, he sat the lumpy pillowcases down just outside the closet.

"There you go, a mill, now get the fuck out my house," Fear spoke to him like he wasn't shit.

"There's been a change of plans." When he said this, Fear instantly became furious, clenching his fists. "I want it all, every last dolla."

"That wasn't the deal," he said through tightened jaws.

"Well, I'm breaking it." Whack! Broli struck him on the side of his head, dropping him down to his knees. "I don't wanna see or hear about chu even touching crack, ya hear me? That isn't your hustle anymore, find yourself a new one 'cause should I catch wind that you're still out here doing you, I'ma kill you, ya understand?"

"Fuck...fuck you!" Fear winced down on his knees, rubbing the side of his head.

Broli kicked him in the ribs and when he doubled over, he was rewarded with the butt of the gun slamming into the back of his skull. Fear hit the floor on the side of his face snoring, having been knocked out cold.

An hour later

"Uhhh...uhh." Fear groaned and grimaced coming out of his unconscious state. His head was pulsating and his vision was blurry. He felt the back of his head again and came away with dry blood. Slowly, his vision came into focus and he looked up at the safe. Suddenly, he forgot about his headache when he saw that he had been cleaned the fuck out. There wasn't a dollar left inside. It was as clean as a whistle. Fear grabbed a hold of the safe door and pulled himself to his feet. He gave the safe another scan just to make sure that he wasn't overlooking anything. Once he saw that he was indeed broke, he slammed the door of the safe and kicked it violently. "Shit! Shitt!

Shittt!" He swung on air, hands looking like blurs while in motion.

"Alvin! Alvin!"

"Italia?" He looked alive hearing his name being called. He darted out of his bedroom and stopped at the head of the steps. Looking down, he saw his lady still handcuffed to the guardrail. "Hold up, baby." He hurried down the staircase and headed into the two car garage where he grabbed a saw. When he raced back inside of the condo, he saw the rod that his girl had been cuffed to until it came loose. As soon as she free, she threw herself into his arms and he hugged her lovingly. "You, okay, babe?"

"Yes, are you?" She looked up into his face.

"Nah," he shook his head no, glassy eyed and shit, "That dirty mothafucka cleaned me out." He balled his hand into a fist and it bulged with veins. Gritting, he slammed his fist into the wall behind him, knocking a hole in it.

"It's okay, I got like, three hundred thousand saved you could flip…"

"I'm through with that game."

"What chu mean?" She frowned.

Fear went on to explain to her what had happened that night between he and Broli as well as the law that he'd laid down about his hustling.

"Well, what're you gonna do?" She questioned, caressing the side of his face.

Fear shut his eyes and took a deep breath, blow out hot air. He felt defeated, but what could he do? His head was on the chopping block. Suddenly, he remembered something else that he'd always been good at doing. His eyelids peeled apart and he locked eyes with his soul mate.

"I got it, I got it." He said in his eureka moment. "Throw on something; I need you to take me somewhere."

"Okay." Italia got halfway up the staircase before he was calling after. She turned around to him raising an eyebrow.

"Get whatever money that chu have stashed, alright?"

"Alright." She continued up the staircase and disappeared inside of the master bedroom.

Fear circled the couch and plopped down. Leaning forward, he rested his elbows on his knees and steeple his hands underneath his chin in contemplation. Closing his eyes and exhaling, he realized that he didn't have a choice in the matter he had to do what he had to do. The action that he was about to take wouldn't be too far a leap from his current occupation. It wasn't like his hands weren't already stained in blood. Shit, he was already condemned to spend an eternity in hell, so it wasn't like he wasn't like anything he did now would change the route in which his soul was heading.

"Okay, I'm ready," Italia called from the staircase as she came running down them.

"You got my guns?" Fear stood to his feet.

"Yeah." She nodded a little out of breath, holding up the gun case that housed both of his Glock .9mms.

"Good. Let's get the fuck outta here." He headed for the door removing his cell phone from his pocket. Italia had just pulled out of the garage when the person he was calling picked up.

"Sex, I need you to meet me at Hahn 's in two hours. I don't have time to explain, just be there, family," Fear spoke into his cellular. "I love you, bro, peace." He disconnected the call and slipped his cell back inside of his pocket. Afterwards, he took a deep breath and slid down in his seat.

"Hahn's?" Italia asked to make sure.

"Yeah, later though, first we're hitting all my stashes houses," Fear told her. Then he went onto inform her about the move he was about to bust. While he was telling her exactly what it was that he was up to, she didn't seem to have bat an eyelash. "Look, if you with me cool, but if you not, I understand 'cause this is a different level of the game. With that being said, where is yo' head at with it?"

"I'm down for you to the very end."

"I salute cho gangsta."

Fear interlocked his fingers with hers, brought them to his lips and kissed them tenderly. He smirked at her and laid his head back against the headrest, staring out of the window as they continued their journey. Where they ended up next would completely change the course of his life. Nonetheless, it was a move that he felt had to be made.

***

Big Sexy sat in the backseat of an unmarked car talking on his cellular phone. The hood of his hoodie protruded slightly over his head, casting a shadow that kept most of his face in hiding. The only identification of it being him was his signature thick, nappy beard which he'd occasionally comb with a natural fork.

" Alright, my nigga, I'll see you there. I love you, too, peace." He disconnected the call and took a deep breath, running his hand down his face. Stashing his cellular inside of the pocket of his hoodie, he continued to comb out his beard. "This shit is all fucked up, man; I can't believe I did this shit. Snitching? That ain't what G's do." He sucked his teeth and shook his head shamefully, having become what he despise the most.

"Aye, aye, look at me." The man called over his shoulder, looking at him through the rearview mirror from the driver's seat. The husky man's eyes met his through the reflection of the mirror. "You did what chu had to do, you hear me? You didn't have a choice. It was either him or you. Shidddd, if I was in your shoes, I woulda did the same thing. Hell, for that matter, I'm sure he would have to." He looked out of the driver's side window, watching the streets through the tinted glass.

"You think so?"

"You bet cha motha's ass. This game don't have no loyalty, homeboy," he told him reassuringly, eyes still focused on the outside. "You can love her but she won't love you back, believe that."

"I can dig it." Big Sexy nodded his understanding. He knew what he had done was some foul ass shit, but at least he was going to walk away a free man after all of the deception. It was a cold world. If it wasn't for this cheese eating mothafucka, Broli wouldn't have gotten the photographs of all of the dirt that Fear had done.

"What did our friend say?"

"He's headed to Master Hahn 's."

"Hahn ?" The mysterious man's brows furrowed. He narrowed his eyes as he tried to figure out exactly where this Hahn stood in Fear's life, but he came up with nothing.

"He's a martial arts teacher," he informed him, still combing out his beard. "He's been training him since he was a lil' nigga."

"What chu think he's gonna do there?"

"I don't know. I mean, nothing much. Hahn is an old ass man; there isn't much that he could want with him."

"Right, right, right," he nodded his head continuously.

"I did my part, can I get that now?"

"Yep, a deal's a deal," his voice changed as he leaned over into the passenger seat, opening the glove box. He pulled out a file and passed it to the backseat. Through the rearview mirror he watched Big Sexy, who was his confidential informant, flip through the documents inside of the file. "Satisfied?"

"And these are the original documents?" He questioned, trying to make damn sure. He'd sold his best friend out for what was inside of that folder and he wanted to make sure he'd gotten his just due.

"Yes, all of the originals, just like we agreed," he assured him confidently.

"Good, I'm outty." He opened the door and hopped out. Crossing the parking lot of the park he was inside of, he set fire to the pointed end of the file and watched the flames devour it. Seeing half of it engulfed, he tossed it inside of a trash can as he passed it, glancing back over his shoulder. "Bitch ass nigga." He pulled the drawstrings of his hoodie and enclosed it around his head, tying it up. Next, he stuck his meaty hands inside of his pockets and went on about his business.

Back in the unmarked car

"Bitch ass nigga." Broli laughed, picking up the extra file that was lying on the front passenger seat. He'd taken out this one along with the one he'd given Big Sexy. The crooked mothafucka made duplicates. "Hahahahahaha!" he laughed heartily, slapping his knees. Afterwards, he wiped the tears from the corners of his eyes, sat the file aside and cranked up his vehicle, driving off.

Meanwhile

Fear pushed open the door of Hahn's store. The bell hanging over the door chimed as he crossed the threshold. Japanese Folk music played softly in the background. He turned to the bronze life size statue of Buddha and rubbed its belly for luck. This was something he'd done every time he'd entered the store. Fear turned away from the statue and inhaled the inviting scent of Jasmine incents. Closing his eyes and tilting his head back, he took a good whiff before taking in the full scope of the establishment. The place was dimly lit and its shelves and display cases were fully stocked. It was like a liquor store, boutique, weed clinic and antique store all in one. Come to think about it, the place resembled that store that Gizmo was bought at in the Gremlins movie.

Hearing someone approaching at his left, he looked to find Hahn approaching from the backroom. He advanced in his direction taking puffs of an antique pipe that looked like it had been stolen from a museum of Asian artifacts. At first Fear thought it was tobacco, but the aroma expelling from the pipe gave him second thoughts. A whiff of its stench confirmed it for him. It was Kush. The old man was definitely smoking some high quality, top-shelf shit.

"What is it that I can do for you, Alvin Son?" He and Fear bowed to one another. After the pleasantries were exchanged, the old man brushed past him, in step towards the door. Fear stated his business as he watched his teacher lock the door and turn the Open sign over to its Close side.

"I need you to teach me any and everything you know about killing," he told him straight up, looking him square in the eyes. "I need to obtain the skills you had when you were putting niggaz on their backs for Gustavo. Train me, Master, train me to be an assassin like you were."

Hahn took the pipe from his lips and blew out a cloud of smoke. "Why do you need these set of skills? Tell me, Alvin Son, are you in some kind of trouble?" He paced the floor as he listened to Fear. His head was tilted downward so that he'd be focused on the floor, occasionally taking draws and causing smoke to waft around him like he'd just done a magic trick.

"So I've gotta leave the game behind and search for another means to run a checkup. So I figure why not do something I familiar with?"

"Hmmm," he stopped in his tracks, sucking on the end of the pipe and stroking his beard with an unkempt hand. "I'm afraid I can't..."

He was stopped short once Fear dumped the Reebok duffle bag's contents out on the counter, stacks upon stacks of money came tumbling out. Hahn looked pleased when he saw all of the racks that had spilt on the glass counter top. The old man couldn't help but wonder how much it was scattered out before him.

"That's a hunnit and fifty grand for your troubles. And don't tell me you don't need the money. You've come down with cancer, right? When we talked I could tell that you were worried about leaving them with a lil' bit of nothing. Well, here's something. If you train me then it's all yours, every penny of it. That I assure you."

Hahn shut his eyes, took a very deep breath and then exhaled. Peeling his eyelids open, he went to deny Fear but felt a stinging inside of his chest. He grimaced and coughed into his palm. Taking his hand away, he saw the sticky blood there. A length of red saliva hung from his lip to his palm.

"Ah, shit." He curse having seen the blood, the cancer had begun its work on him.

"Master Hahn , I..." A worried Fear lifted his hand and approached, but his teacher raising his hand stopped him.

"I'm fine, I'll be okay." He looked at the pipe in his hand and became enraged, throwing it aside. Next, he wiped the blood off on his clothing. "Okay, you've got yourself a deal."

"Master Hahn , I think you should..."

"I did not ask for your opinion!" His eyebrows arched as he growled. "Now do you, or do you not want this deal?"

Fear took the time to calm himself down, closing his eyes for a moment and slightly nodded. Once he peeled his eyelids back open he said, "Yes, I do."

"Alright then, we leave tomorrow at dawn, deal?" He extended his scrawny old hand, his bony fingers lingering in the air.

His protégé firmly grasped his hand, shaking it. "Deal."

To Be Continued...
Fear My Gangster 2
Coming Soon

Submission Guideline

Submit the first three chapters of your completed manuscript to ldpsubmissions@gmail.com, subject line: Your book's title. The manuscript must be in a .doc file and sent as an attachment. Document should be in Times New Roman, double spaced and in size 12 font. Also, provide your synopsis and full contact information. If sending multiple submissions, they must each be in a separate email.

Have a story but no way to send it electronically? You can still submit to LDP/Ca$h Presents. Send in the first three chapters, written or typed, of your completed manuscript to:

LDP: Submissions Dept
Po Box 870494
Mesquite, Tx 75187

DO NOT send original manuscript. Must be a duplicate.

Provide your synopsis and a cover letter containing your full contact information.

Thanks for considering LDP and Ca$h Presents.

BOW DOWN TO MY GANGSTA

By **Ca$h**

TORN BETWEEN TWO

By **Coffee**

BLOOD STAINS OF A SHOTTA **III**

By **Jamaica**

STEADY MOBBIN **III**

By **Marcellus Allen**

BLOOD OF A BOSS **V**

By **Askari**

LOYAL TO THE GAME **IV**

LIFE OF SIN

By **T.J. & Jelissa**

A DOPEBOY'S PRAYER **II**

By **Eddie "Wolf" Lee**

IF LOVING YOU IS WRONG... **III**

LOVE ME EVEN WHEN IT HURTS **II**

By **Jelissa**

TRUE SAVAGE **VI**

By **Chris Green**

BLAST FOR ME **III**

A BRONX TALE

By **Ghost**

ADDICTIED TO THE DRAMA **III**

By **Jamila Mathis**

LIPSTICK KILLAH **III**

CRIME OF PASSION **II**

By **Mimi**

WHAT BAD BITCHES DO **III**

KILL ZONE **II**

By **Aryanna**

THE COST OF LOYALTY **II**

By **Kweli**

SHE FELL IN LOVE WITH A REAL ONE **II**

By **Tamara Butler**

LOVE SHOULDN'T HURT **III**

RENEGADE BOYS **II**

By **Meesha**

CORRUPTED BY A GANGSTA **III**

By **Destiny Skai**

A GANGSTER'S CODE **III**

By **J-Blunt**

KING OF NEW YORK III

By **T.J. Edwards**

CUM FOR ME **IV**

By **Ca$h & Company**

GORILLAS IN THE BAY

De'Kari

THE STREETS ARE CALLING

Duquie Wilson

KINGPIN KILLAZ II

Hood Rich

STEADY MOBBIN' **III**

Marcellus Allen

SINS OF A HUSTLER

ASAD

HER MAN, MINE'S TOO **II**

Nicole Goosby

GORILLAZ IN THE BAY **II**

DE'KARI

TRIGGADALE II

Elijah R. Freeman

THE STREETS ARE CALLING **II**

Duquie Wilson

Available Now

RESTRAINING ORDER **I & II**

By **CA$H & Coffee**

LOVE KNOWS NO BOUNDARIES **I II & III**

By **Coffee**

RAISED AS A GOON I, II, III & IV

BRED BY THE SLUMS I, II, III

BLAST FOR ME I & II

ROTTEN TO THE CORE I III

By **Ghost**

LAY IT DOWN **I & II**

LAST OF A DYING BREED

BLOOD STAINS OF A SHOTTA I & II

By **Jamaica**

LOYAL TO THE GAME

LOYAL TO THE GAME II

LOYAL TO THE GAME III

By **TJ & Jelissa**

BLOODY COMMAS I & II

SKI MASK CARTEL I II & III

KING OF NEW YORK I II

By **T.J. Edwards**

IF LOVING HIM IS WRONG…I & II

LOVE ME EVEN WHEN IT HURTS

By **Jelissa**

WHEN THE STREETS CLAP BACK I & II III

By **Jibril Williams**

A DISTINGUISHED THUG STOLE MY HEART I II & III

LOVE SHOULDN'T HURT I II

RENEGADE BOYS

By **Meesha**

A GANGSTER'S CODE I & II

By **J-Blunt**

PUSH IT TO THE LIMIT

By **Bre' Hayes**

BLOOD OF A BOSS **I, II, III & IV**

By **Askari**

THE STREETS BLEED MURDER **I, II & III**

THE HEART OF A GANGSTA I II& III

By **Jerry Jackson**

CUM FOR ME

CUM FOR ME 2

CUM FOR ME 3

An **LDP Erotica Collaboration**

BRIDE OF A HUSTLA **I II & II**

THE FETTI GIRLS **I, II& III**

CORRUPTED BY A GANGSTA I & II

By **Destiny Skai**

WHEN A GOOD GIRL GOES BAD

By **Adrienne**

A GANGSTER'S REVENGE **I II III & IV**

THE BOSS MAN'S DAUGHTERS

THE BOSS MAN'S DAUGHTERS II

THE BOSSMAN'S DAUGHTERS III

THE BOSSMAN'S DAUGHTERS IV

THE BOSS MAN'S DAUGHTERS **V**

A SAVAGE LOVE **I & II**

BAE BELONGS TO ME

A HUSTLER'S DECEIT I, II

WHAT BAD BITCHES DO I, II

By **Aryanna**

A KINGPIN'S AMBITON

A KINGPIN'S AMBITION **II**

I MURDER FOR THE DOUGH

By **Ambitious**

TRUE SAVAGE

TRUE SAVAGE II

TRUE SAVAGE **III**

TRUE SAVAGE **IV**

TRUE SAVAGE **V**

By **Chris Green**

A DOPEBOY'S PRAYER

By **Eddie "Wolf" Lee**

THE KING CARTEL **I, II & III**

By **Frank Gresham**

THESE NIGGAS AIN'T LOYAL **I, II & III**

By **Nikki Tee**

GANGSTA SHYT **I II &III**

By **CATO**

THE ULTIMATE BETRAYAL

By **Phoenix**

BOSS'N UP **I , II & III**

By **Royal Nicole**

I LOVE YOU TO DEATH

By Destiny J

I RIDE FOR MY HITTA

I STILL RIDE FOR MY HITTA

By **Misty Holt**

LOVE & CHASIN' PAPER

By **Qay Crockett**

TO DIE IN VAIN

By **ASAD**

BROOKLYN HUSTLAZ

By **Boogsy Morina**

BROOKLYN ON LOCK I & II

By **Sonovia**

GANGSTA CITY

By **Teddy Duke**

A DRUG KING AND HIS DIAMOND I & II III

A DOPEMAN'S RICHES

HER MAN, MINE'S TOO

By Nicole Goosby

TRAPHOUSE KING **I II & III**

KINGPIN KILLAZ

By **Hood Rich**

LIPSTICK KILLAH **I, II**

CRIME OF PASSION

By **Mimi**

STEADY MOBBN' **I, II**

By **Marcellus Allen**

WHO SHOT YA **I, II**

Renta

GORILLAZ IN THE BAY

DE'KARI

TRIGGADALE

Elijah R. Freeman

GOD BLESS THE TRAPPERS I, II, III

THESE SCANDALOUS STREETS I, II, III

FEAR MY GANGSTA I, II

THESE STREETS DON'T LOVE NOBODY I, II

Tranay Adams

THE STREETS ARE CALLING

Duquie Wilson

Tranay Adams

BOOKS BY LDP'S CEO, CA$H

TRUST IN NO MAN

TRUST IN NO MAN 2

TRUST IN NO MAN 3

BONDED BY BLOOD

SHORTY GOT A THUG

THUGS CRY

THUGS CRY 2

THUGS CRY 3

TRUST NO BITCH

TRUST NO BITCH 2

TRUST NO BITCH 3

TIL MY CASKET DROPS

RESTRAINING ORDER

RESTRAINING ORDER 2

IN LOVE WITH A CONVICT

Coming Soon

BONDED BY BLOOD 2

BOW DOWN TO MY GANGSTA

Fear My Gangsta

CPSIA information can be obtained
at www.ICGtesting.com
Printed in the USA
LVHW011547150921
697894LV00010B/1088